# Resurrection

# By Danielle Steel

# DANIELLE STEEL

# Resurrection

*A Novel*

Delacorte Press

New York

Published in the United States by Delacorte Press, an imprint of Random House, a division of Penguin Random House LLC, New York.

DELACORTE PRESS is a registered trademark and the DP colophon is a trademark of Penguin Random House LLC.

Hardback ISBN 978-0-593-49846-0
Ebook ISBN 978-0-593-49847-7

Printed in the United States of America on acid-free paper

randomhousebooks.com

2 4 6 8 9 7 5 3 1

First Edition

To my beloved children,
Beatrix, Trevor, Todd,
Nick, Sam, Victoria,
Vanessa, Maxx, and Zara,
so greatly loved!

May you be safe and blessed,
strong and whole,
and cherished by those
who love you.
May they love you
as much as I do!

With all my love,
Mom / d.s.

# Resurrection

# Chapter 1

Darcy Gray always put the finishing touches on her blog, The Gray Zone, on Sunday nights, after she'd let it sit for a few days. She liked to take a last look. She posted it on Mondays, and enhanced it with daily posts on Instagram to introduce additional ideas and products she supported. She had started her blog for fun, thirteen years ago, at twenty-nine, when her fraternal twin daughters Zoe and Penny had started kindergarten. It had been the perfect activity for a full-time, hands-on, at-home mom. She had introduced it before blogs were commonplace, and she used it to share her views about upcoming fashions and trends, her opinions on a variety of subjects, research on new health and scientific information. She treated it like a letter to friends. It had gone viral almost immediately, and for more than a decade she had been one of the most respected bloggers and influencers in the country, and even around the world. Her readers trusted her. Her opinion was sought by magazine editors, companies, and trendsetters of all kinds.

In the years since Darcy began writing The Gray Zone, influencers had become a powerful force in the world of promotion and communications. Companies and major brands sought the attention of major influencers to endorse their products and paid as much as twenty-five thousand dollars for a single post, which could add up to a multimillion-dollar business for a blogger like Darcy, one of the most respected in the business. It was a highly desirable job now.

Darcy was sought after for her authenticity—she never wore, used, or recommended a brand or product she didn't believe in, and her followers had total faith in her. She never let them down or led them astray for her own gain. Blogging and influencing had become a new way for companies to engage directly with individuals and communities on a personal level to promote their products. Darcy had been among the first to catch that wave to success. Her sincerity, good taste, and good judgment shone through every word.

As the only daughter of the head of a distinguished publishing house in New York, and her mother an editor, Darcy had always wanted to write. She just didn't know what until she started The Gray Zone.

Because of her parents' involvement in publishing, they had always pushed her in that direction. They were convinced that she had talent as a writer and encouraged literary ambitions at a lofty level. They hoped she would be an important novelist one day and tried to instill that desire in her. She had been an English literature major at Princeton, which had been her parents' wish for her. It was her father's alma mater.

Since her parents had been unable to have children for the first twenty years of their marriage, Darcy had been a late, happy surprise. Her father had hoped for a son to follow in his footsteps at Princeton, and into the literary world. Instead, Darcy had agreed to go to Princeton when she was accepted, but she had her sights set on modern pursuits, and her writing aspirations went no further than the internet while she was in college.

The disadvantage she found in having older parents—her mother was forty-six when she was born, and her father ten years older— was that they were overprotective, and old-school in all their views of the world. Both from New York families, venerable and distinguished but with diminished funds, they wanted Darcy to live in their own familiar world, but she was of an entirely different generation and mindset, she was an independent, free-thinking young woman, and her parents' lofty literary world held no appeal for her. It seemed like a relic of the past.

In their dreams for Darcy, they imagined her following a path similar to their own, working for ten years as a writer or editor in publishing and marrying someone like them one day, with the same goals and interests. Instead, Darcy had met Charles Gray in her junior year at Princeton, through a mutual friend. Ten years older than she, not long out of Columbia Business School, Charlie was following his own unusual dreams, and was determined to make his mark in the world of retail fashion, where he could see there were fortunes to be made. His ideas were exciting and made sense to Darcy. She hadn't found her own career path yet, but she was sure that he would go far with the plans he explained to her. She loved how modern and ambitious he was.

They had in common the fact that they were both only children of older parents who had set ideas for them. Charlie's parents were originally from Boston. His father was in banking, and his mother had never worked. His parents couldn't understand his fascination with the world of retail and would have preferred to see him go into banking like his father. Charlie wanted to own department stores, which made no sense to his parents.

Both sets of parents felt strongly that Darcy and Charles should seek solid jobs working for other people, for salaries they could count on, that their romance could simmer for a decade, and that they should not rush into anything.

Youth won out in the end. Charlie proposed to Darcy the Christmas of her senior year, and despite their parents' reservations, they were married in June. Their parents were shocked even further when Darcy got pregnant on their honeymoon, with the twins. In their parents' opinion, they were moving with lightning speed, without careful planning.

The other thing Darcy and Charlie had in common was that they both had parents who were old-fashioned in their views of marriage. They were of a generation that was reserved, as their own parents had been and had modeled for them. They showed little emotion to each other, or even to the children they loved. Charlie and Darcy were excited by each other's bright minds, and his visions for the future, but at first they were more comfortable talking business than showing overt signs of affection. They had no role models for an affectionate, playful marriage. It was a meeting of the minds and both of them had been shy for a long time about being open with their feelings. It was their daughters who warmed them up eventually and taught them to love more openly. Both Charlie and Darcy recognized that their similar upbringing hadn't served them well in teaching them to have a loving, demonstrative relationship. It was unfamiliar to them. They loved each other deeply but didn't show it easily.

It came as no surprise to Charlie or Darcy when they lost both sets of their parents within the first decade of their marriage, in a period of two years. Darcy's mother was seventy-seven and died of a heart attack in her sleep. Her father, at eighty-seven, had a stroke months later and had been in frail health for several years. Both of Charlie's parents had died of cancer at seventy-five and eighty, and his father had had severe Alzheimer's. It left the twins without grandparents, and had been a hard, sad two years as the grandparents died in rapid succession one after the other. Charlie and Darcy supported each other through it. Their parents' final years hadn't been easy, for them or their children. It made Darcy grateful that she and Charlie had had their own children when they were at a much earlier age, and were young parents. With nineteen-year-old daughters in college, they were younger now than their parents had been when they were born. Darcy and Charlie still had years ahead of them to have fun and enjoy their lives and pursue their careers, which they both thoroughly enjoyed.

Thirteen years after she started The Gray Zone, at forty-two, with a husband and twin daughters, and over a million followers, Darcy still loved doing it. She had a widely heard voice on many subjects, not just fashion. She was invited to exciting events all over the world and had an extremely lucrative business. Both her fraternal twin daughters had started college a year early, at Boston University, and were juniors now at nineteen, and were studying abroad for a year. Penny, a tall, lanky dark-haired beauty with blue eyes, who closely resembled her equally striking mother, was studying at the University of Hong Kong. She was an econ major, with a minor in fashion merchandising, and wanted to work for her father at his flagship department store in New York, one of his four stores, when she graduated. She had a calm, quiet, sensible nature. Penny had studied Mandarin in high school and college, and was speaking fairly fluent Cantonese now, after five months in Hong Kong, since September. She felt that speaking Chinese would be useful in business, and for working with the factories her father dealt with for their exclusive lines at the stores. She was living in a luxurious apartment her parents had rented for her in The Peak section of the city, with three female roommates. Unlike their own parents, Charlie and Darcy were supportive of their daughters' ambitions and dreams.

Zoe, Penny's younger twin by seven minutes, was as different from her sister in looks as she was in personality. Petite, with an elfin air about her, she had long straight blond hair, big green eyes, and looked like her father and his side of the family. Her father, Charles Gray, was tall, and as blond as Zoe was. She looked like her paternal grandmother. Zoe had a fiery personality and took any difference in opinion from her own as a personal affront. She got along better with her father than with her mother most of the time, but not always. She was studying art history at the Sorbonne in Paris and had a particular interest in the Impressionists. Her dream was to get a job as a curator at the Metropolitan Museum in New York. Darcy was on the board of the Met's Costume Institute, and Charlie was on the board of MoMA, so the family was well connected in the art world.

Zoe had fallen in love with a young medical student almost as soon as she got to Paris in September. Jean-Paul Thibaut, twenty-six years old and the adored only son of two doctors, was studying at the Faculté de Médecine. He was staying at Zoe's tiny, quaint Left Bank apartment most of the time in the Saint-Germain-des-Prés area in the 6th arrondissement. She had found it on the internet herself, and was now speaking fairly decent French, thanks to Jean-Paul.

Charles and Darcy had met Jean-Paul during one of their visits to Paris and liked him, but hoped the relationship didn't get too serious too quickly. They wanted Zoe to come back to the States for her senior year, like her sister, Penny, and graduate from B.U. Zoe was already talking about taking graduate classes in France after her senior year. She had a mind of her own, and was much less compliant than Penny, who was having fun with her three roommates in Hong Kong, and more intent on her studies than on romance, which was typical of her. Zoe took life by the horns, and lived it fully, even at nineteen. Penny was more cautious.

After marrying Charles as soon as she'd graduated from Princeton and getting pregnant with the twins immediately, once they were born they kept Darcy too busy to even think about a job for the first few years, and Charlie was content to have her stay at home to take care of their babies, while he built his retail empire. Then she started the blog, which filled her time, eventually brought its own rich rewards, and allowed her to be a full-time mother until the twins left for college. Darcy had never wanted another job. Writing The Gray Zone suited her perfectly, although it had been a mystery to her parents for several years. But Charlie had encouraged her to write it. As a major influencer, she had an enviable position now. Her previews about fashion and all the information she shared in the blog were well chosen and well informed.

When they had first married, Charlie, with an MBA from Columbia, had turned a modest amount of inherited family money from his grandparents into a booming success in retail. Twenty-five years before, while still in business school, he had realized that there was big money to be made in fashion and had bought a small failing department store in downtown New York with a group of investors he'd gone to business school with, and as they branched out into other investments, and once he could afford it, he had bought them out. An important group of Hong Kong investors had subsequently helped him build a highly lucrative chain of four high-end luxury department stores in New York, Chicago, L.A., and Dallas. He ran them all from his home base in New York, with "Gray's" in New York as their flagship store.

Gray's Department Store had a reasonable online business, but the real appeal for its customers was the brick-and-mortar experience and excitement of visiting the stores. They were magnificently merchandised with extremely profitable results. They made many of their own exclusive items, some fabricated in China for bigger margins, and others in Italy, especially their high-quality, high-style leather goods. If you wanted gorgeous bags and shoes and accessories, you went to Gray's. They bought high-priced luxury lines in Paris and carried all the most important American and foreign designers of the day.

Charlie's success had allowed him to buy a handsome townhouse in the East Eighties early in their marriage, and the house in South-ampton shortly after, put his daughters through the best private schools in New York and one of the best colleges, and lead a very comfortable life. Charlie and Darcy were invited to every major so-cial, charity, and fashion event in New York. They were important people to know.

They were a good match and had a solid marriage. They had both grown with their success. They enjoyed each other's company, and were equally busy, constantly attending important events, and Char-lie traveled a great deal to China, Italy, and France. Paris was always Darcy's preference, while Charlie spent more time in Milan and Rome, keeping an active eye on the Italian lines they bought. The store's fashion director was French, so she traveled more frequently to Paris. Charlie was a hard worker and kept a hand on every aspect of the business. And he frequently asked Darcy's advice. Their great-est competitors now were the shopping opportunities on the inter-net, but Charlie still believed that a real live store was king and had its own special magic, and he hadn't been wrong so far.

Undeniably, two major careers ate up a lot of Charlie and Darcy's waking hours. There were weeks when they hardly saw each other. They tried to spend quality time together but couldn't always. Darcy was as busy as he was and wished she had more free time. They managed to be together more once the girls left for college, although he traveled more than ever once they were gone. Knowing that Darcy was busy too, he felt free to travel to Italy twice a month, and to China regularly. Darcy's real job now was as an influencer of brands of all kinds. She had a powerful voice, and could make or break the creators and individual companies she wrote about on her blog. People begged for her attention, and she was modest about it, but the reach she had across the internet was huge.

Charlie was hands-on about his business and visited his stores outside New York regularly. They never knew when he'd show up, between trips to Europe and Asia. Even his employees loved their stores. They loved working there and the merchandise they sold. He was a good man to work for, a creative and financial genius and a fair boss. The stores were holding their own against their internet competition. Charlie's stores were a model for success. They had come through a world crisis four years before stronger than ever, after the Covid-19 pandemic in 2020.

Darcy was proud of him and their twenty-year marriage. They had celebrated their twentieth anniversary in New York, and she was planning a little surprise for him. It was always a challenge for them to find time to be alone together and really talk and relax. She knew better than anyone that you had to grab the moments together when you could. Sometimes the best moments for them were when he was on the road. They'd shared some wonderful trips in the past. With the girls gone now, she had no need to be tied down at home. She was free, and wanted to take advantage of spending more time with him. He was a moving target, often traveling.

Charlie had left for Italy the day before. He was starting in Rome, to meet with the managers of the factories he worked with there, and then heading for Milan, which was one of her favorite cities too. Darcy knew he was planning to stay on for fashion week in Milan. She was going to visit Zoe in Paris on the way home, and attend Paris Fashion Week, while Charlie stayed in Italy to oversee their orders and meet their biggest buyers. His fashion director was going to Paris while he worked in Rome.

Darcy was leaving for Rome the next day to surprise him and only planning to stay a few days in Italy, or for as long as Charlie's schedule would allow. She knew how busy he got on the road, entertaining clients, meeting with important established designers and new ones. He could make a designer successful just with the orders he placed for his stores. A big order from Charlie could make a young designer a star overnight.

Charlie always attended fashion week in Milan, while Darcy was more inclined to attend fashion week in Paris, and sometimes they were like ships passing in the night, which was why she had decided to surprise him in Rome. She'd been planning it for weeks. Even if he was busy, she could join him for dinner at night. Rome was romantic at any time of day. They loved traveling together when they had the time. She was excited about leaving New York the next day on the early flight to Rome. She smiled, thinking of it. It was going to be fun! And a little romance in a twenty-year marriage never hurt.

Their relationship had been strong for all the years they'd been married, although they weren't always demonstrative with each other. Darcy accepted that about him. Their parents had been that way too. And over the years, she and Charlie had warmed up. Above all, they had a deep respect for each other, and what they had each achieved. Charlie was proud of Darcy, and she admired him. His acquiring Chinese investors so he could make his operation grow into four beautiful, successful stores had been a stroke of genius, and challenging for him. His entrepreneurial talent was one of the things that had attracted Darcy to him in the first place and that she admired most about him. And even though he loved his business, he was a devoted husband and father, and she was a good wife and they loved each other.

He had built his retail empire before most people were seeking partners and investors in China. She had watched him make the business successful store by store, and with the sizable influx of Chinese money, he had been able to do what he could never have done alone.

Their daughter Penny recognized that too, which was why she wanted to work for him and learn how he ran the business. She was more interested in finance than in fashion. And she hoped one day to convince him to enlarge their online component, to compete with all the online brands that didn't have a high overhead, because they didn't have a physical store to support. She knew how much his stores meant to him, but the future was coming and things were going to change. Charlie wasn't convinced of that yet, but Penny was sure he'd see it one day soon. He was too smart not to.

Charlie was a powerful, handsome man. He was fifty-two years old, ten years older than Darcy, but looked more like he was forty. He played squash at the Racquet Club twice a week, usually with business associates, and tennis once a week at their Southampton house with friends. He was always on the move and stayed in amazing shape. Darcy kept him aware of healthy foods and products and important medical trends, which he attempted to follow as best he could, traveling as much as he did. He was always on a plane to somewhere, most often to Italy. It was the foreign country where he felt most at ease, and at home, other than the U.S.

Darcy liked to say that their marriage was a well-oiled machine that ran on schedule and never went off the rails. She was highly organized, and they both lived by schedules, Charlie's being dictated by the fashion calendar with set seasons and his travel schedule. Darcy was aware that there wasn't enough romance in their life, but that was the inevitable casualty of two careers as successful as theirs. Their working life was important to both of them. And the lack of romantic moments in their marriage didn't bother her. The love and respect in their marriage was more important to her than flowers and frills that she didn't need or expect from him. She had realized it when their daughters were in high school, and between the girls' needs and the demands of her blog, and Instagram, the research that went into it, and the constant meetings she had with important brands who paid for her support, she and Charlie hardly ever saw each other. She had vowed to improve that after the girls left for college. But even then, once the girls had gone, she and Charlie often had trouble making their schedules mesh.

With the surprise trip to Rome, she was making a concerted effort to meet him where he was, bring a little romance to him, and show him that she cared. He knew she did, but there was so little time to demonstrate it. What better way than a few romantic nights in Rome? Even if he was rushing to fashion week in Milan right afterward, and she was hoping to see Zoe for a few days before she attended Paris Fashion Week, which was always an important event for her work. Her stop in Paris was going to be a surprise for Zoe too. She was afraid that if she warned her, Zoe might let something slip when she spoke to her father and spoil the surprise in Rome. So only Darcy and her travel agent knew that she was flying to Rome the next day. She loved the idea of surprising him. She hadn't done anything like that in years. But he'd been too busy to give her his schedule, and his assistant in Rome said it changed constantly, so she wasn't sure when he'd have free time. She decided to surprise him in Rome anyway and adapt to whatever free time he had. His schedule in Rome this week seemed the least likely to be overbooked.

Milan was always much busier, as the Mecca of Italian fashion, and closer to the factories he worked with. His younger, newer designers that he helped develop were often in Rome. The big established firms were in the north in Milan, or the factory towns around it. The factory area around Milan had been the hardest hit in the pandemic four years earlier and had taken time to reorganize and get up and running again. It had slowed production down for a while, but everything had been back to normal for three years now. Italy had suffered enormous losses, and had recovered well. Charlie seemed busier than ever now in Italy.

The pandemic had happened when the girls were in high school, in their junior year, and had taken major organizing to keep their studies on track while they were preparing to apply to college in the fall. Everything had been back in order for their senior year, but their junior year had been a nightmare, with a world health crisis, and a two-month quarantine. Keeping teenagers isolated at home had been the greatest challenge, and Darcy had managed to keep her Instagrams and blog active, informative, and interesting in spite of it, offering helpful positive suggestions about how to get through the crisis. Charlie had been in Asia when it happened, and it had been complicated getting home, and then he had to quarantine for two weeks without seeing any of them when he returned. But they'd been careful and lucky, and none of them had caught the virus. There was a vaccine for it now, and all of them had had it, as had people all around the world. They had all been assured that it couldn't happen again, and if somehow it did, it would be a far weaker strain of the disease and wouldn't bring the world to a screeching stop the way the last one had. It had been the strangest time of their lives, almost like a nuclear attack on every country on the planet.

Darcy, Charlie, and the children had taken refuge at their house in Southampton for the pandemic while New York blazed with the dreaded virus. Darcy lost a number of friends to it, and Charlie did as well. Teenagers got it less frequently, but a few of the twins' friends caught it, with no fatalities. It really had been the most awful, anxious-making time of their lives. All the stores had been closed, nationwide, Charlie's among them of course, and he had paid his employees full salary to stay home for two months, which had nearly bankrupted him, with no income from the stores. His longtime Chinese investors and government bailouts had helped him, and he had righted the ship afterward. They were more profitable than ever now, and it was all a dim memory. But it had been a terrible time for the whole world.

In the four years since, there had been a kind of celebratory atmosphere, a new joie de vivre and abandon to pleasure. People loved each other more, were more demonstrative, more expressive about their feelings, spoiled themselves and each other more readily, traveled and spoiled themselves more afterward, which was great for Charlie's business. Everyone seemed to take greater pleasure and satisfaction in living, and the knowledge that it couldn't happen again, once the vaccine was found, was reassuring. It was a kind of delightful delirium. People had sex more readily. More babies were born than previously. People got married, bought dogs, took vacations, smiled at their neighbors and strangers on the street. Every day was a celebration of life and freedom, once they were no longer confined, which in part was what had inspired Darcy to surprise her husband with a quick visit to Rome while he was working. She was excited as she closed her suitcase, slept for a few hours, and got up early the next morning. She couldn't wait to see the look on his face when she arrived in Rome and surprised him in his hotel room at the Hassler. She smiled thinking about it. They needed more spontaneous time together, and this would be it.

She had booked a car and driver to take her to the airport. She checked in for her international flight, happy that she didn't have to wear a mask while traveling anymore, although a few people still did.

She had a fruit salad and a yogurt in the first-class lounge, and boarded the plane, as the flight attendants greeted her and escorted her to her seat. She'd brought some things with her that she had to read for her clients. She had promised herself she wouldn't work in Rome. She was going to soak up the atmosphere of the city, shop, visit churches, and walk around while she waited for Charlie to finish his appointments. She knew he would be happy to see her. Charlie loved surprises, more than she did. She liked organizing every minute and planning things ahead so everything would go smoothly. Charlie was a little more free-form and relaxed about things, when he didn't have meetings back-to-back, and she hoped he wouldn't. It was going to be fun, and afterward she would see Zoe in Paris before the shows of fashion week, which kept her running all day.

The plane took off, and she saw Manhattan disappear beneath

them as they headed across the Atlantic. She resolved to do things like this more often. She and Charlie needed to be more playful, and put a real spirit of romance back in their life. They'd never had enough of that, having had the twins so soon after they got married. And she had been on bed rest for five months before they arrived and couldn't leave their bedroom or her bed. For the last nineteen years, she and Charlie had always been too busy working to spend much time together, juggling their careers, trying to be good parents, doing everything they were supposed to do. It was time now to loosen up and have some fun. Neither of them had elderly parents to take care of anymore. And with the girls studying abroad for junior year, their burdens and family obligations were lighter. It was time to make room for each other, and relax. They had the money to do it, and now they had to make an effort to focus on each other.

She watched two movies, ate a sumptuous Italian meal on the flight, and took a nap. When she woke up, they were landing in Rome. The fun was about to begin! She was so glad she had decided to surprise him! She thought it was the best idea she'd had in years, and would add spice and romance to their marriage, which was always a good thing.

# Chapter 2

When Charles Gray arrived in Rome, Flavia Tedesco picked him up at the airport as she always did, in her ridiculously tiny Fiat 500, which was fine since he only traveled with carry-on and no luggage. Flavia was a startlingly beautiful thirty-three-year-old designer with a halo of loose reddish blond curls. Her family had dominated Italian fashion for generations, with her very well-known father Umberto as the current head of the empire. She had a brother, Roberto, and two sisters, Stella and Bianca, in the family business as well. Roberto handled finance, Stella designed shoes and handbags, and Bianca sportswear and swimwear. Their mother ran PR. Their older brother Pietro had been next in line to run the company, and had died in the coronavirus epidemic, as had his wife, an aunt, an uncle, and two cousins. Italy had been hard hit.

Flavia had started her own line of clothing three years before, and Charlie had shot her into the public eye with a massive order when he saw her first show in Milan. The alliance had proven fruitful for them both, and they had worked closely together to successfully launch her line. She had enormous talent, and he knew her family well too. He was particularly fond of her father, who was in his seventies now, and ran the business with an iron hand. Flavia's father was very proud of her independent success, and grateful to Charlie for his active role in it.

As she drove Charlie into the city, they talked rapidly, catching up on news. She was as stylishly dressed as ever, wearing one of her own new designs. When she needed something new to wear, she whipped something up and had her studio make it. She was wearing an armload of beautiful bracelets, some of which he'd given her, and she glanced at him and smiled, happy to see him. He had been in Rome two weeks before, but his absences always felt like an eternity to both of them.

She was a major success in Europe, and Charlie had made her a success in the United States too. She did beautiful daywear and exceptional evening gowns. Each one was special and had an haute couture look to it. She had her own distinctive style, and her customers and Charlie's couldn't get enough of her clothes. Fashion editors loved her designs and her natural elegance. Her clothes sold for high prices in his stores' designer departments. She had an exclusive with his stores in the States, which had worked out well for both of them. They talked mostly about work on the way into the city.

She drove him straight to her home in the Colli Aniene area of the city, with a view of St. Peter's. They went to her house, as they always did, so he could drop off his carry-on bag before he went to the office with her. He kept a suitcase of old clothes at the Hassler Hotel, which they put in a room for him during his reservation, just to keep things looking respectable, although he never slept there. He had a buying office in Rome, to keep track of the company's orders in Europe. It was in the same building as Flavia's office now, which was convenient for them both. He had to stop off at the Hassler Hotel too, to check in. He used the room for personal deliveries and messages. He hadn't used the room there in the past two years, but he left the suitcase there so they could put it in his room.

Charlie stayed with Flavia and had a European cellphone to use in Rome. When they first worked together, they had been careful not to let their feelings run away with them. The attraction was palpably there, despite the nineteen years between them. He had made it clear that he was married and loved his wife. But things had subtly changed between him and Darcy over the years, the busier she got. They were best friends, and consulted each other on business matters, but the romance had long since gone out of their relationship. It had just seeped away, and he didn't know when it had happened. He hadn't even noticed it, as the twins got older and kept her busier. Between the girls and Darcy's ever more important work as an influencer, there was never a spare moment in her day for him or anything else. He was busy too, and traveling constantly, in the States and abroad. He was home less and less frequently, without realizing it, dealing with a problem at a factory in Europe or one of the stores in the States. There was no time to connect, warm up, and little tenderness between them. He had learned to live without it, and then suddenly meeting Flavia had brought him back to life and reminded him what it felt like when a man and a woman connected on every level.

It was rapidly obvious that it was more than just physical attrac-

tion between him and Flavia, although that had been like an electri-
cal current that jolted him back to life in ways he had forgotten. But
the love she shared with him and lavished on him was like rain on a
garden that had lived through a drought. He was starving for everything she had to offer him, and she had never known anyone like
him. He was thoughtful and giving and caring. Every moment they
had spent together had been a joy, and still was. Their relationship
was constantly deepening and growing.

When he went home to Darcy, after being with Flavia, Charlie realized that the essence of their relationship had slipped past them
while they were busy with everything else. He readily admitted that
Darcy had made more effort than he did to keep their marriage alive.
But whatever they'd done hadn't been enough. Neither of them had
noticed that the life force had gone out of the marriage, and it was
dead. Only their bond over their daughters had kept it alive. He
didn't know when desire had left them, but it had, for a very long
time. They'd been too busy to notice.

Flavia had exploded into his life with all the bright lights and excitement of fireworks. He respected Darcy, but he fell deeply in love
with Flavia. It had all become impossible to resist on a trip to India
to buy textiles together. Every moment between them had been magical, then and ever since. He hadn't expected it. He had no intention
of divorcing Darcy and breaking her heart, but he could no longer
live without Flavia. She was the air he breathed, and the blood in his
veins. And she never asked him to divorce. She understood his situation and accepted it with the utmost respect. The fact that she didn't
ask brought them all the closer, and now, in the past three months

since November, everything had become more intense. He hated leaving her at all, even for two weeks.

He put his arms around her and swung her off her feet when they got to her house, which was stylishly decorated like everything else she touched. She had set up a home office for him, and had everything the way he liked. She always made time for him no matter how busy she was. Charlie was her priority in a way he never had been to Darcy. But Flavia also didn't have teenaged twins to deal with, only him. She was a brilliantly talented designer, and the woman of his dreams. He had no idea what the future would look like, but he knew how much he loved Flavia, and also how much he owed Darcy for standing beside him for twenty years. He didn't want to hurt either of them, and had no idea how to avoid it. So he had made no sudden moves, and lived every moment to the fullest with Flavia.

Her family knew what was going on. Her father turned a blind eye to it, out of his long-standing respect for Charlie in other ways, but he was worried about his daughter. Her brother Roberto was more outspoken. He and Charlie were good friends, and Roberto told him in no uncertain terms that he should get divorced and marry Flavia. She told Charlie to pay no attention to him, it was none of his business.

The coronavirus pandemic four years before had changed everyone and made everything more precious. It had raced through Italy like a forest fire, before Flavia started her business, and she met Charlie a year after it ended. Losing her older brother in the epidemic had inspired her not to wait any longer to pursue her dreams, and she had branched off on her own then, as Italy was rebuilding.

Her father had given her his blessing to go out on her own, for the same reasons. Life and time meant more than ever before, and one never knew how much of either one had left. It had been the right decision for her, and she felt that the relationship with Charlie was too. And now another element had been added to bind them even closer together.

They made love as soon as they got home. She made him lunch afterward, before they left for the office, stopping at the Hassler on the way, so he could check in, in case Darcy called him there. It was a courtesy to her that he still paid for a hotel room every time he was in Rome, although he lived with Flavia, and had for two years. They had reached a comfortable point in their relationship with a certain stable reliability to it. They didn't advertise the fact that they lived together, in deference to Charlie's situation, but their intimates and her family knew.

When they had time, they made short trips to Venice, Lake Como, Puglia, London, Paris. He always explained that Flavia was there to advise him on their collections, in the coming season. She had come to New York a few times in the last two years, but it was riskier for him there, and they preferred being in Europe together. He didn't want to hurt Darcy, and he knew it would kill her if she found out about them. He had been tormented about it at first—it was his first and only affair, and a very serious one, and now more than ever. They were having a baby in August. It had been an accident, but he couldn't repress the profound happiness he felt about it. Everything she did made him happy, and he knew their baby would too. They had decided together to proceed with the pregnancy. And as soon as they did, and he guessed, her brother Roberto began to hound Charlie about a divorce, which Flavia did not. Her father didn't know about the baby yet, but Flavia was a grown woman, and she knew he would accept her choice, whether he approved or not. He ruled the family as he did his business, but he respected Flavia as an intelligent, honorable woman, and Charlie as an equally honorable, responsible man.

She had no regrets about the baby. Others she knew had similar arrangements, with children out of wedlock. Working together was a joy for her and Charlie, and having the baby would be a bigger one, an even stronger bond.

After they showered and dressed and had a quick lunch in her sleek modern kitchen, they got back in Flavia's tiny car, and this time Charlie drove. They made a handsome couple, both blond. Flavia was tall with a model's body and soft titian strawberry-blond hair. Her mother was Florentine, and it was a familiar hair color there, as were her big green eyes. She smiled as Charlie slid into the Roman traffic, which made him feel like a race car driver. It had taken him years to get used to it, and now he loved it. He loved the lively streets and atmosphere of jubilant chaos of Rome. It was so different from the life he had led growing up. His parents had been serious and conservative. Overt demonstrations of affection made them acutely uncomfortable. They were originally from Boston and had moved to New York, when Charlie's father became the head of J.P. Morgan when Charlie was seven. Flavia's exuberant Italian family would have shocked them. They were much more at ease with a family like Darcy's New York social register parents. They had always liked her and approved of the marriage.

"Don't forget we're having dinner at my father's house tonight,"

Flavia reminded him. "I think everyone will be there." The family congregated regularly, either to discuss new business plans or simply enjoy a meal together. He loved their big noisy Roman family, with their father presiding and their mother fluttering around, enjoying being surrounded by her children, as many as possible. They had an enormous dining room and kitchen to accommodate everyone.

"We should tell your father about the baby soon," Charlie reminded her gently. "Do you want me to tell him?" he offered, and she shook her head and ran a light hand through her curls.

"No, I will, at the right time. When I'm alone with him." Umberto pretended not to know they lived together but she knew from her older sister Stella that he did. He just didn't want to have to acknowledge it and put the heat on Charlie. He figured that Charlie and Flavia were old enough to work it out for themselves. Their nineteen-year age difference didn't bother him at all. Umberto was in his late seventies, older than Flavia's mother Francesca. The fact that Charlie was married was a bigger problem, one that he hoped Charlie would ultimately resolve whatever way he felt was right. Unlike his son, Umberto thought it was best to let Charlie decide how to handle it. He felt sure that Charlie would do the right thing in the end. He was that kind of man. He was surprised that Charlie hadn't so far, since he'd been so obviously in love with Flavia for two years, but Umberto could easily imagine that the situation was complicated. They appeared to be sublimely happy. It always pleased Umberto to see them together. And given his age and personality, Charlie brought a degree of seriousness to the situation, and obviously didn't take the relationship lightly. Umberto was a man of the world, and he wasn't shocked by it. All he wanted was a good outcome for Flavia. She never seemed to be suffering when her father saw her, or even when he didn't, according to all reports from her mother and siblings.

"Well, don't wait till it shows," Charlie said. She had wanted to wait until their three-month sonogram, when they would be assured that everything was normal, which was scheduled for the next day.

"I won't, and don't forget that we have the sonogram tomorrow."

"I know. I wouldn't forget that." Everything had been so high-tech and medical, fraught with worry, when Darcy was pregnant with the twins. She had gone into early labor several times and they'd been able to stop it with modern science. The twins still came a month early, but they were healthy, which was all that mattered. With Flavia, everything was so easy and so natural. It was just beginning to show at three months when she was naked, and he loved the gentle early small swell of her belly. He could hardly wait to see their child. "Do you suppose they'll be able to tell us the sex at the sonogram?" he asked eagerly.

"Maybe, depending on the position. Otherwise, I had a blood test, and they'll be able to tell us in a couple of weeks." She and Charlie had debated about whether or not to let it be a surprise, but they had both decided they wanted to know. "Maybe I'll wait to tell my father until we have those results, or if we can see it on the sonogram tomorrow." And then she remembered something she'd heard on the news, which concerned her. A chill had run down her spine when she heard the report. It was fleeting but worried her, and she meant to tell him about it, to see what he thought. Charlie was always sensible, intelligent, and levelheaded.

"I heard a crazy warning on the news the other day, about a new virus, supposedly a distant cousin of Covid-19. It's supposedly not as dangerous, or as lethal, but highly contagious, and resistant to the Covid-19 vaccine." Nearly everyone around the world had had the vaccine by now, and had it yearly. The very mention of the virus that had caused the pandemic four years before struck fear into people's hearts. It had been short-lived but had infected many millions and killed seven million people worldwide. The Tedescos' own family losses had been heavy, including Flavia's older brother, his wife, an aunt and uncle, two cousins, and many people they knew. The toll was high in every country. The vaccine was discovered in two months and until then it had taken a heavy toll, and was an agonizing memory. The pandemic had lasted for about two years, and trickled away slowly for months afterward. Charlie had lost several of his business associates in Asia, a few close friends in New York, and a number of employees. Fortunately, neither he nor Darcy nor the twins had gotten it. But the reverberations in economies around the world had been felt heavily for a year. It had originated in China and had created havoc around the world. Charlie had come very close to losing his stores, but a government bailout and his investors in China had saved him.

"You don't suppose it could happen again?" she asked him. It had come so close to home with her that she was more worried than Charlie.

"For one thing, lightning doesn't strike twice in the same place," he said calmly as he drove, darting in and out of traffic. "And I don't think anything like it could ever happen again. Governments would jump on it much faster if there were a next time. In 2020, they didn't know what they were seeing and there was no way to stop it by the time they did. They have very specific protocols now if it rears its ugly head again, or even something like it, and we have the vaccine now, which made a big difference. People may still get it, but they won't die of it, unless they have other illnesses."

"They say this virus isn't as bad, but it's distantly related to Covid-19, and there's no specific vaccine for it yet. A lab in Thailand reported on it, and they've seen some cases in Japan." He could see that she was worried about it, and even more so because of the baby.

"Just be careful," he said gently, pointing to her belly, "and if you're concerned, follow the same protocols we used then—keep your distance, wash your hands, and if you travel or go to a big gathering, wear a mask."

"People will think I'm crazy." She smiled at him. "The pandemic ended two and a half years ago. No one does all that anymore."

"If there's a new virus afoot, it won't hurt to be careful. But it will never get to the proportions of Covid-19. That just won't happen. Something like that happens once in a century, maybe, like the Spanish flu, or once in a millennium." She nodded, wanting to believe him, but it had worried her anyway. Nobody would ever have believed that the coronavirus would reach the proportions it did. It had been the worst in China where it started, and in the United States where it ended, and had ravaged every other country in between to varying degrees. People had been confined to their homes for months, businesses were closed and many eventually lost, borders were closed for several months, planes were grounded. No one could ever have foreseen the magnitude it reached. "It won't happen again, Flavia." Italy had been the third hardest hit on the spectrum, but the researchers had been vital in helping both to discover the medicines which worked to fight the virus, and ultimately the vaccine, which had proven to be effective in reducing the severity and the risks. And the strains that still existed were much weaker and rarely fatal. There hadn't been a single reported case in the world in more than three years.

"Some people always said it would come back," she said softly, hoping it wasn't true, "or some mutation of it."

She wanted to believe Charlie's reassurance, but she was still anxious about it. The memories of those awful months were still too vivid, especially since they had lost her brother Pietro, and his wife Marcella. Fortunately, they had had no children to be orphaned, but she missed her brother sorely, and knew her parents did too. They all did. He had been the funniest of her siblings, the smartest, and the kindest, and the closest to her father. Oddly, Umberto was closer to Flavia rather than Roberto, now that Pietro was gone. Roberto and his father frequently argued about the financial side of the business. Roberto thought their father was too old-fashioned. And Umberto thought his son spent too much money and lived beyond his means.

Flavia was quiet for a time as she thought about it while they drove to the office. "There are no cases in Europe yet," she added, "it's all in Asia, but it could come here, just as Covid-19 did, and maybe just as quickly if it's so contagious. I don't think they know much about it." It was all so familiar, like the kind of vague reports they had in the early days with Covid-19, when no one had guessed yet how dangerous it was.

They had stopped at the Hassler briefly so he could check in, and reached their office building by then, and had other things to think about. Charlie needed to meet with his staff and see what troubleshooting he had to do. There was always some situation that he had to deal with, and Flavia had design meetings all afternoon.

She left him at his office, lingering for a moment to kiss him, with the door closed. They were an open secret, but they both preferred to maintain a certain level of decorum. People knew that they were dating, but not that he lived with her, or that they were having a baby, although they'd see it soon enough. The baby was due in six months, but it would be apparent eventually no matter how cleverly she tried to conceal it with her ingenious designs. At a certain point, a healthy pregnancy was impossible to hide. And she didn't really want to. She was proud of their baby. But she still wanted to maintain a professional demeanor and avoid showing it off for as long as possible. Especially since her father didn't know yet, nor did her mother. Her sisters had guessed almost immediately. They knew her too well and had been pregnant too often themselves to miss the signs. They had three children each. Their mother was oblivious, and always worrying about Umberto. She thought he worked too hard, but the business was his life force and what made him seem vital and youthful. He was a handsome, elegant man.

"I'll come upstairs to see you later," Charlie promised, fully engaged in the hours ahead. His assistant had his list of appointments ready for him.

As soon as Charlie arrived in Rome, he felt as though he had never left. This was where he belonged now. His life with Flavia seemed centered and grounded, even more so than his life in New York.

In Rome, he had a woman who worked in the same business, who was fully aware of the challenges he faced daily, and talked them over with him at night. He never felt alone here, or lonely, which happened to him frequently in his life with Darcy. It took too long to explain it all to her, and she was always too busy. But she gave him good, sound business advice when he asked for it, which he didn't do often anymore. He had Flavia to talk to now, and he took full advantage of it. He called her several times a day from New York too. His life flowed from Rome now. It no longer felt like a visit. It felt like home to him because Flavia was there. His world revolved around her, and hers did the same with him. They fit together like two pieces of a puzzle, and had since the day they'd met. They had long since admitted how much they needed each other, and how much better their life was now, because the other was in it. What they had found was a rare gift, and whatever the conditions or circumstances they had to live with and adjust to, neither of them doubted for a single second that it was worth it. And Charlie knew that one day he'd have to deal with Darcy. He knew he would, but he wasn't ready to yet.

# Chapter 3

Umberto and Francesca Tedesco lived in a beautiful Roman villa that had been in the family for three generations. It was in an elegant neighborhood on Gianicolo, one of the seven hills of Rome. As an only son, Umberto had inherited it from his parents, and his children had grown up there. It had beautifully sculpted gardens and an ornate stone façade. There had been lots of room for his five children, and Roberto still stayed with them occasionally when he wanted to be waited on, although he had a very chic bachelor pad, a penthouse apartment in the Parioli area of Rome. But he liked staying with his parents too, and his mother loved it. It was not unusual for single Italian men to keep one foot in their parents' homes until they were married.

Roberto had had a string of beautiful girlfriends, mostly actresses and models, and none of them marriage material. He was thirty-eight years old and in no hurry to marry and interrupt his fast-paced Roman bachelor life. He was the fourth child of the five. Pietro had been forty-two when he died in the pandemic, and would have been forty-six now. Stella was forty-one, Bianca was thirty-nine, and Flavia was the baby at thirty-three. Their mother Francesca was sixty-seven years old and from an aristocratic Florentine family. Umberto had the look and profile familiar on a Roman coin. The Tedescos were a handsome, impressive group when all together. Stella's husband Massimo was an attorney, and Bianca's husband Paolo was in advertising. Neither of them worked in the family business, but all of the siblings did, and they were an effervescent, ebullient group, talking and laughing, and occasionally arguing about the business. They were very close, and often spent vacations together at their house in Sardinia. It was rare for any of them to vacation separately, although it happened once in a while. Stella and Bianca's husbands would have liked it to happen more often, but didn't dare suggest it. The Tedescos liked being together all the time, and were vocal with their opinions about each others' spouses, children, houses, friends, and latest designs.

Francesca handled public relations for the firm, making sure that their clothing was well represented and always in evidence around the world, worn by movie stars and celebrities, presidents' wives and royalty. The company had a head of marketing, and had hired younger people to handle social media for them, since it wasn't part of Francesca's generation, but she was a wonderful ambassador for their line. Her own family wasn't involved in fashion, but Umberto had gotten her involved in the business early on. He liked having her near at hand. He was seventy-eight years old now, a very handsome man, and Francesca was still a beauty even now in her sixties. Flavia looked a great deal like her. Stella, Bianca, and Roberto had their father's raven-haired good looks. They were noticeable wherever they went, tall, handsome, aristocratic, and elegant. They had a natural gift for style.

The Tedescos were always laughing and talking and gesticulating. Charlie loved being with them. As an only child, they were the siblings he had never had and wished he did. He had known Pietro better than the others and got to know the others better after he died. Once he and Flavia started working together, he got to know them really well.

He and Flavia's sisters got on well, and he carried their lines, as well as Flavia's, at all his stores. Tedesco was a major international brand. Flavia's designs were a little more luxurious and haute couture, and also higher-priced and more fashion-forward, than Bianca's designs for the family brand. Bianca would have loved to work for her sister, but their father would never have tolerated another family member leaving the home brand. He had recognized early on that what Flavia wanted to create didn't quite fit the family mold, and he knew she was and always would be frustrated working for him. She had started working for him when she finished design school at twenty-three, did her best for him for seven years, and was thrilled when he set her free at thirty to start her own line. He had lent her the money to start her own company.

He had learned that lesson during the pandemic. Pietro had always been frustrated working for his father, who had him placed as their head of finance. For years Pietro had wanted to start his own avant-garde menswear line, which would never have worked with the Tedesco label, so Umberto hadn't let him. Pietro, as the oldest son, had loyally done what was expected of him, but never what he dreamed of and enjoyed, and then he died so young. Umberto didn't want the same fate for Flavia, who had such definite ideas about what she wanted to design, so when the pandemic was over he opened the door wide to let her pursue her dreams as she wanted. He had shown her early designs to Charlie, who had a major market for them in the States, and the rest was history.

She was a big success now. Umberto hadn't expected them to get involved romantically. It had never occurred to him, and he was startled when he realized that they had more than a business relationship, but he admired Charlie, and was hoping he would eventually leave his American wife and become his son-in-law. He felt sorry for Charlie's wife, but lives and people changed, and it was obvious to Umberto that Charlie's marriage must not have been fulfilling, when he saw how close and happy he and Flavia were. A good marriage did not leave room for a relationship like that to flourish elsewhere. He had had his own dalliances when he was younger, just brief passing fancies, but never serious ones, and he had been faithful to Francesca for most of their forty-seven years together. She was a good woman, a great mother, and a wonderful wife. They exchanged a smile across the dinner table, as their children gathered and shared a lavish meal. Francesca knew how to make everyone happy and keep a lovely home. She added light and beauty to everything she touched, and each of their children had their own style and did honor to the family name.

Francesca's mother still lived in Florence and was ninety-three, living on her own in their family's palazzo with three ancient family retainers who were almost as old as she was. Francesca visited her two or three times a month, and her older sister, who didn't work, lived near their mother and visited her every day, so they knew that she was well cared for. She was still beautiful at ninety-three, impeccably dressed in the clothes Francesca sent her since she hated to shop, with her hair freshly done, perfectly manicured red nails, and the beautiful jewelry she still wore. They called her Nonna Graziella, and she was the only grandparent the Tedesco children still had. Her own family palazzo was filled with spectacular Italian Renaissance art. She had been a widow for nearly fifty years and was content living alone, with daily visits from her oldest daughter, who was widowed too.

They were a close-knit family in every way, each one with their own distinct personality. Roberto was fun, outgoing, loved women. He was outspoken and spoiled, and Flavia said he was too good-looking for his own good. Women fell at his feet. He was like a bee flitting from flower to flower with no desire to settle down. Stella, his older sister, had a strong voice. She was never afraid to stand up to their father, and she thought she would run the company better than her brother one day, but Umberto didn't agree with her and was hoping that Roberto would grow into the role, maybe once he married and settled down in a few years.

Stella was a talented designer and made beautiful shoes and bags of the highest quality, and she worked well with Bianca, her next younger sister. Bianca was more docile than any of the Tedescos. She was the peacemaker in the family, and her clothing designs kept the brand current without ever stepping over the line with anything too outrageous. She made Tedesco garments wearable for many years without ever going out of style, and she was thoroughly enjoying designing their new swimwear line and had sought Flavia's advice about it. Flavia had given her some great ideas for playful one- and two-piece suits, and Stella had designed sandals and straw bags to go with them. They became the latest craze, and the company couldn't produce them fast enough to fill their orders.

Flavia got along with all of them. She knew when to dodge Stella if she was on a rampage about something, or fighting with their father or Roberto. Stella stirred the pot and kept things lively, and viewed Flavia as her baby sister, since she was eight years older. She had been the first to guess about Flavia's pregnancy, recognizing the signs. She was happy for her, but like Roberto, she was eager for Charlie to straighten out his life and marry her. Although many young people in their circles had babies out of wedlock these days, they were a traditional family with old-fashioned values, marriage being one of them. She and Bianca had both married young and had their babies after they were married. Pietro had married early too, but Marcella hadn't been able to have children, and they didn't want to adopt. Pietro didn't want to bring up someone else's children, and Marcella had made her peace with being childless and was wonderful with the nieces and nephews. It had been a tragedy for all of them when they both died, within days of each other, from the virus that had devoured Italy and the world.

The family had a relaxed lively evening and were talking about fashion week in Milan at the end of the meal, when Roberto slid into the chair next to Charlie that Stella had just vacated to check on her children, who were watching TV in the library. She had three sons who were avid soccer fans, and Bianca had two daughters and a son.

"So? When's the wedding? Before she gets too big, I hope," he said softly, with his usual subtlety and a devilish grin.

"You're five years older than I am, Berto," Flavia said in a whisper. "It would be rude of me to get married before you do. So, when's yours? What about that sixteen-year-old starlet I saw you with last week in the paper?" Flavia shot back across Charlie, sitting between them. Their parents were at the other end of the table so they couldn't hear them.

"She's not sixteen, she's nineteen. She wants to be a doctor."

"She looks thirteen. Has she met Mama and Papa yet? You have to bring her to dinner. She can play with Bianca's kids," who were younger than Stella's. Roberto and Flavia loved to provoke each other. "Leave Charlie alone. He comes here for a decent dinner, since I can't cook, not to listen to you harass him. He doesn't make rude comments about your love life."

"I haven't gotten anyone pregnant," he said, looking virtuous.

"Yet. That we know of. And when you do, she'll probably be a cocktail waitress or a stripper."

"Those girls know better."

"Oh, don't be so full of yourself." Charlie let them throw barbs at each other, while he finished his tiramisu and coffee and tried to finish a conversation with Stella's husband, Massimo. He had seen a report on the new virus too.

"I'm not sure if we should panic or not. It was one of those sensational headlines that usually don't have much behind it," Massimo said.

"I'm starting to worry," Bianca said, frowning, "if it's true. I never know what to believe. They told us it would never happen again once we had the vaccine, so it can't be true," she said, glancing at her husband, Paolo, who nodded, agreeing with her. Massimo wasn't as sure.

"This is supposedly a distant cousin of Covid-19," he volunteered, "but this one isn't responsive to the vaccine."

"I think it's just nonsense," Stella said when she returned and ousted Roberto from her chair. "They just want to scare us. The government would never let it happen again."

"I hope you're right," Charlie said quietly, held Flavia's hand under the table, and smiled at her.

The evening ended on an upbeat note as it always did. They left shortly after midnight. They had only started to eat at ten P.M., after having arrived at nine.

Charlie drove himself and Flavia home. There was still plenty of traffic, there always was in Rome. Like New York, it was a city that never slept. The cafés were full until late, the bars and restaurants too. People sat at tables, talking for hours. People loved to talk in Italy, and eat, and be with their families and friends, and walk along arm in arm, winter or summer.

It had been a nice evening. Charlie always enjoyed the time he spent with Flavia's family, and he liked both her brothers-in-law. He'd had a chance to talk to Umberto about a factory he was thinking of buying north of Milan. He had radically cut down their use of Chinese factories in the last few years, after the pandemic. Charlie didn't bring up the subject of the new virus again. It was disturbing that a number of people had heard about it, and it was hard not to dredge up the memories of Covid-19, even if this one was allegedly less dangerous. He hoped the rumors about it died out quickly.

"Do you have a big day tomorrow?" Charlie asked Flavia as they got ready for bed, and he smiled when he saw her gently rounded belly.

"We're finishing our fittings for fashion week. For once, we're ahead of schedule. And all of our fabrics came," she said, as she slipped into bed next to him.

"I can't wait to see the new collection." They would be showing the summer line, and she was happy with it.

He lay on his side, gazing at her. She was so beautiful—her face was flawless and her hair looked like angel curls. Every time he saw her he wondered how he'd gotten so lucky. He hoped they'd have a little girl who looked just like her.

She snuggled up next to him, and they fell asleep. She was happy he was home again.


When Darcy arrived in Rome, she didn't want to spoil the surprise and call Charlie. She went straight to the Hassler, where he always stayed. They recognized her name when she identified herself as Mrs. Charles Gray, and gave her a key to the room, even though they didn't know her. She looked extremely respectable and well dressed and they didn't doubt she was who she said she was. She hadn't been to Rome in almost two years, so she wasn't familiar to them. If she met Charlie in Europe, it was almost always in Paris. He told her that he preferred to keep Italy strictly for work, and they'd have more fun in Paris, especially now with Zoe there.

When she got to his room, she was surprised by how small a room he had these days. He certainly didn't spoil himself or have much space to move around. When they traveled together, they took suites in the best hotels, which the Hassler was, and she had stayed there with him before, usually in a large suite with a terrace and a splendid view of Rome and the Spanish Steps. The furniture and upholstery were pretty in the room he had this time, but it was much too small for two of them. Alone, she supposed it didn't matter, since he was out at meetings all day, and had business dinners every night. She'd gotten to the hotel at dinnertime, and he was out.

She was tired and didn't bother to order room service. She helped herself to some sparkling water in the minibar and opened a can of nuts. It was all she wanted for now. She had eaten on the plane. With the time difference from New York, she lost a whole day traveling, but they would go to sleep when he got home, and she'd be fresh and rested the next day, and could shop and walk around while he worked. She was looking forward to having some time with him, and he might even manage a free evening once he knew she was there.

She walked around the small room, opened the closet, and saw he hadn't hung anything up, although he'd left New York two days before she arrived. She saw his very small rolling carry-on suitcase on the floor next to the desk, and decided to unpack it for him since he obviously hadn't had time. She opened it and there were two shirts and a suit in it, carefully folded, socks, and some papers. It certainly wasn't enough for the two weeks he planned to be there, but he obviously must use the hotel laundry on a daily basis, and he was wearing another suit, since he was out. It certainly wasn't a generous wardrobe for the two-week trip, but men had a way of making do with less than most women would take for a weekend.

Darcy had brought two good-sized suitcases, which instantly crowded the room before she even opened them. There were always more shoes than she really needed, both high heels for the evenings, and low heels for walking around Rome, a pair of tennis shoes, several handbags to go with different outfits. An extra coat since it was February, a peacoat, and a dressy jacket for the evening in case he took her someplace nice. There was no way she could have managed with less, especially since she was planning to go to the fashion shows in Paris, and the press always photographed her and kept track of what she wore and how she dressed. She was something of a celebrity in the fashion world.

She hung Charlie's suit in the closet and put his shirts on a shelf. He must have only brought the shoes he was wearing since there were none in the rolling bag. He had really been Spartan on this trip. She hadn't paid attention to what he packed in years, but it was no wonder he complained about her luggage when they went somewhere. Two suits, two shirts, and a single pair of shoes was definitely bare bones, but men were lucky that way. They never needed different shoes for every outfit and a matching bag. She smiled as she finished the nuts and thought about ordering a sandwich while she waited. She turned on the TV to CNN, sat down in a comfortable chair, and fell asleep. She never got out of her clothes, and woke up at seven the next morning. The sun was streaming into the room, and the bed hadn't been slept in. Charlie hadn't come back to the hotel, and she had no idea where he was, or if something had happened to him.

She got undressed and put on a terrycloth robe hanging in the bathroom, wondering if she should be panicked or if there was some reasonable explanation for it. She knew he wasn't a cheater, but he could have had an accident. She called his cellphone and it went to voicemail. She left him a message, and then went to take a shower, and ordered coffee and toast. It was almost nine o'clock by then, and she was getting seriously worried when she heard a key turn in the lock, and Charlie walked in, looking neat and clean and freshly shaven. He looked like he'd seen a ghost when he saw her. He had come to get some papers from his bag. They had been there for months, and now he needed them.

"What are *you* doing here?" he asked her, shocked.

"Where were you all night?" she answered.

"Um, I had a meeting outside Rome to look at a new factory. The owner invited me to dinner at his home. It got late, we had a lot to drink, and he invited me to stay in his guest room so I didn't have to drive back." She knew it had to be something like that, but she'd been worried anyway. "What are you doing in Rome, Darcy?" he asked her, stunned.

"I wanted to surprise you." She smiled at him, walked over, and gave him a hug, her worry now dispelled. "I thought maybe we could steal a fun weekend somewhere before Milan Fashion Week, after your meetings in Rome this week. Maybe Lake Como? Or Florence?" She looked excited and hopeful, and he tried to look pleased, but he wasn't. He was panicked—he and Flavia had planned a ski weekend in Cortina that they'd both been looking forward to. Darcy's unexpected arrival put a serious kink in his plans. She had never done anything like this before, and he had no idea why she would now. "I thought it would be fun to surprise you," she said, not noticing that Charlie hadn't even kissed her. He was amazed to see her.

"That's very sweet of you," he said with the tone you'd use with an ancient aunt who had knitted you an ugly sweater you knew wouldn't fit and didn't want. His double life had finally caught up with him. "But I have such a busy week, I wish you'd asked me, or warned me. I have business plans every day and night. I don't have time to entertain you or spend with you." He sounded firm and was panicked.

"You don't have to," she said calmly, "I can find plenty to do on my own. What are you doing tonight? Maybe I could join you." He felt sick as he realized what the next week was going to look like, and how he was going to explain it to Flavia. He would tell her the truth of course, but she wasn't going to be happy about it. Darcy had never entered into or interfered with their world before.

"Are you going to fashion week in Milan?" he asked, with a sinking heart and rising stomach.

"No, I thought I'd spend the week with Zoe, and then I've got Paris Fashion Week the week after. Are you going to that?" She knew he almost never did, but he never missed Milan. "You could join me and Zoe in Paris, if you can spare the time."

"I really can't. I'll have been here for long enough. I'll need to get back." He could feel a headache starting as he thought about the dinner plans he had with Flavia that night. "Why don't you spend a day here, and then go to Paris early? We can do this surprise trip another time. I just have too much on my plate right now, Darcy. I can't make it work this time at such short notice. You'll have a better time with Zoe." She looked disappointed, but she had realized that he might be too busy, and took the chance. But she didn't want to leave the next day. She loved Rome and wanted to be with him now that she was here.

"Let's see how it shakes out. Don't worry about me. I'll be fine. Just do what you have to do, and I'll see you after. I wasn't expecting you to drop everything for me. I guess surprises in lives like ours aren't always easy to accommodate." She realized now that she hadn't been realistic when she planned the surprise. It had seemed like a good idea at the time.

"Especially the week before fashion week. I'm really sorry." He looked sheepish and genuinely sorry. He hated lying to her, but there was no way he could spend a week in Rome with both women expecting to spend time with him. He had never been in a mess like this before.

"What time are you going out tonight?" she asked him, as he rummaged in his suitcase for the papers he wanted, and found them.

"I'm not sure," he said vaguely, "eight, nine. I'll have to check. People go to dinner pretty late here." He no longer remembered what their plans were that night, Flavia was the keeper of their social schedule. And he couldn't call to ask her. "I'll call you from the office after I check. My calendar is there."

"No worries," she said calmly. Darcy looked a lot more relaxed than he did. He put the papers he'd come for in his pocket, grateful that he'd stopped by the hotel so he at least knew she was in town. "I'll have fun today on my own. I can do some shopping research for the blog." He nodded, looking distracted.

"Fine. And call Zoe and try to work something out with her for this weekend. It's going to be very hard trying to make time to see you, I've got meetings back-to-back." She knew what that was like. He did the same at home, and so did she. It was the story of their life. But in fact, he had a relatively free week ahead so he and Flavia would have time together, something he never did with his wife. He felt guilty about the entire situation, and all he wanted to do now was get to the office and tell Flavia.

He gave Darcy a hug before he left the hotel room he never used. "I'm sorry not to be better prepared for the surprise," he said, feeling awkward. "It was a really sweet thought."

"I'm sorry the timing isn't great for you. I took the chance. Next time we'll plan it together." She smiled, determined to be a good sport about it. She realized that if he landed on her unexpectedly on one of her work trips, she would have been just as flustered as he was. She scheduled her meetings minute by minute too. The surprise trip had been a spontaneous idea, which seemed like fun. She wondered if they could at least salvage a few days together.

"I'll cancel whatever I've got for dinner tonight, Darcy. At least we'll have one evening together before you leave." She nodded, as he left. He was certainly making it clear that he didn't want her to stick around. But she didn't want to call Zoe. She had been planning to surprise her too.

Charlie took a cab to his office and went straight upstairs to Flavia's office as soon as he arrived. He felt like a train wreck and looked like one when he walked into her office. She was about to start a design meeting and was surprised to see him.

"Is something wrong?" she asked in an undertone.

"Yes. Can we talk for a minute?" She led the way into her private office.

"Did something happen?"

"I walked into my room at the Hassler, and Darcy was there. I nearly had a heart attack."

"Your wife? She's in Rome?"

"She came as a surprise. She wants to spend a week and I told her it's impossible. I told her to go and see Zoe in Paris. I think I have to have dinner with her tonight and spend the night with her at the hotel. And I'm going to do all I can to get her to leave tomorrow. But whatever we're doing tonight, I have to cancel."

"There's a party at the Hotel de Russie in celebration of all the Roman designers showing in Milan. It's not a big deal if you miss it, but do you think she'll really leave?"

"She'd better. I don't want her ruining the week for us, and this is a little too close to home. It's like a bad movie."

She smiled at him. "We'll manage. Hopefully, she'll go." He looked awful, she could see how upset he was.

"I'm working on it," he said, looking stressed.

"It's a bit comical," she said, trying to see the humor in it. She could just imagine what her brother would say if he knew, but there was no reason why he should. As long as Charlie got Darcy to leave, it would be fine. Flavia had to go to her design meeting then, and Charlie went back to his own office downstairs.

He was nervous and distracted all day. He almost missed his lunch appointment, and was twenty minutes late. Fortunately, it was with a man he knew well who seemed not to notice. He called Darcy twice during the day, and she seemed happy and fine, visiting churches and doing some shopping. He told her he'd meet her at the hotel at seven and made a dinner reservation at Casina Valadier for eight-thirty. It was an exquisite restaurant. And he sent Flavia three dozen roses to apologize. She stopped by to see him before he left the office, and he was even more nervous than he had been that morning. It was why Flavia didn't go to New York anymore. He couldn't deal with having both women in the same city. It was too complicated, and not a game he wanted to play. He didn't know how some men did it and actually thought it was fun. He didn't.

He kissed Flavia before he left the office and got to the Hassler on time. Darcy was lying on the bed, relaxing, surrounded by a sea of shopping bags, which filled the small room. She didn't want to complain to Charlie and ask for a bigger one. She said she'd had a fun day.

She wore a new dress to dinner that night, and looked very pretty, which made him feel even worse. He didn't want to spend a romantic evening with her, just have a nice dinner and go back to the hotel. He had a splitting headache during dinner, and Darcy could tell.

"Did you call Zoe today?" he asked her, and she shook her head.

"She's not expecting to see me in Paris till fashion week. I was going to surprise her next week."

"You said you'd call her." He looked tense when he said it.

"I'm not staying with her, so all I need is a room at the hotel. I can call her once I'm there. Her schedule isn't as heavy as yours. I might as well stay a few more days now that I'm here. I never get to Rome. I always forget how much I love it." His panic increased as she said it. He wanted to cry. There was nothing funny about this, it was awful. And so was their situation. Having both women in Rome made that very clear to him. Roberto was right. He needed to clean up his life. He just hadn't been planning to do it this week.

He was quiet on the way back to the hotel, and Darcy handed him two Extra Strength Tylenol when they got to the room. She could recognize one of his bad headaches from the look on his face. "You must have had a stressful day," she said sympathetically.

"I did," he said, and took the pills gratefully.

"I'm sorry to add to it by showing up when you're busy. Thank you for dinner, I loved the restaurant."

"I did too. I'm sorry to be such a stress case. I have a lot on my mind."

"It's fine, don't worry about it. Maybe I'll leave on Friday, and you can catch up on work on the weekend," she said, and he almost groaned. Friday was two days away, and he was missing precious time with Flavia that he had carefully planned, to carve out time for them. And now he was juggling both women and enjoying neither. But it was the reality of his life, and he couldn't force Darcy to leave, nor tell her the truth. He fully realized that he richly deserved the headache for creating an impossible situation with a woman he was afraid to hurt by leaving, and felt guilty about having built a whole life with another woman before he did. They were even having a baby now, and he was spending the night in a hotel room with his wife, which was the last place he wanted to be while he was in Rome. He didn't mind sharing the house with Darcy in New York. They came and went and had their own lives. But now she was suddenly infringing on his life with Flavia. He lay awake that night, thinking he had to tell her, with his head pounding, but he couldn't tell her now, far from home, when she had innocently planned a surprise that was blowing up in his face and hers.

Charlie looked exhausted the next morning when he got up. Flavia texted him while Darcy was in the shower, reminding him that the sonogram was that morning, in an hour, and he wasn't even dressed yet.

"Oh my God," he said out loud as he texted her back. "I'll be there. I can't wait to see our baby. I hope it's a girl!" he wrote. She sent him the address, which he remembered, and he rushed into the shower as soon as Darcy got out. "I forgot I have an early meeting," he said to Darcy as he hurried to shower, cut himself shaving, and dressed.

"Do you have time for breakfast?" she asked innocently.

"No, room service is slow here. I'll be late. I can have coffee at the meeting," he said, trying to look cheerful. "What are you doing today? More shopping?"

"Probably." She smiled. "Are you busy tonight?"

"I am, I'm sorry, Darcy. I canceled plans last night. I can't tonight." He needed to be with Flavia to celebrate their baby, especially if they found out what sex it was. He owed her at least that in this totally screwed-up week that wasn't going according to plan at all. And he'd have to find an excuse not to sleep at the hotel.

He kissed the top of Darcy's head, wished her a fun day shopping, and flew out of the room in time to get to the appointment, and had the doorman get him a cab. The doctor's office wasn't too far away, and he sat back in the cab with a sigh and closed his eyes. He was living a nightmare and knew it was all his fault, because he hadn't dealt with it before.

He arrived at the doctor's address just as Flavia parked her car and got out, and they walked into the doctor's office together with his arm around her. She didn't ask him about the night before, and he focused on her and their baby and tried to forget the rest. This was their time now.

Darcy tidied up the room a little after Charlie left. He had draped the shirt he wore the night before over a chair, and she rang for the housekeeper to have it sent to the laundry. She ordered breakfast, using the phone on the desk in the small, cramped room, and noticed that Charlie had forgotten his cellphone and left it on the desk. He never did that at home. His phone was never out of his hand except when he slept, nor was hers. They were an even match, as the classic couple with two big careers. She noticed that he had a phone she'd never seen before, different from the one he used at home, and she picked it up. It sprang to life in her hand and the screen lit up. He kept his phone at home locked, and it needed a code. This phone was wide open, and Flavia's text was on the screen as Darcy looked at it, along with his response. She stared at it for a minute, wondering if it was someone else's phone, maybe the previous guest had forgotten it. It couldn't be Charlie's, but deep in her gut she knew it was.

Flavia had written him "Don't forget the sonogram this morning at nine-thirty," and she'd given him the address of the doctor's office. Charlie had responded "I'll be there. I can't wait to see our baby! I hope it's a girl!" Darcy's eyes blurred with tears then as she read it. Flavia's response had been "See you there. I love you. Ciao." Darcy felt sick as she read it again, and there was no avoiding the fact that it was Charlie's phone. He was going to see a sonogram of a baby, "our" baby, and he hoped it was a girl. How was that possible? She felt like life was moving in slow motion, and her brain with it. He was having a baby with someone, and going to see a sonogram, just like he had done with her twenty years ago when they saw the twins. And who was this woman? How could he have a baby with her, and she not know? Was she deaf or blind that she had never suspected anything? How could she miss that he was having a baby with another woman? She felt stupid and suddenly broken and torn in half, as though someone had dropped her out of a window, and her whole world shattered when she hit the ground, like a piece of glass, into a million pieces. She didn't even know how to pick the pieces up again. She was too shocked and hurt to be angry. She felt traumatized and numb. She was in shock, too much so to react. And suddenly she realized they were at the sonogram now. If she wanted to know who the woman was, she could see them when they left the doctor's office, if she hurried. She wanted to know, to see her face, to see him with her so she'd know if this was real or some cruel joke. Suddenly she had to pull herself together to get there in time.

She grabbed a pair of black jeans out of her suitcase, and a sweater, put on the flat shoes she'd worn the day before, quickly brushed her hair haphazardly, grabbed her coat and handbag, and ran out the door. Her breakfast hadn't come yet—he was right, room service was slow. All that mattered now was that she get there in time to see them so she would know who the enemy was and what she looked like. This might be her only chance.

She felt like a crazy person as she had the doorman get her a cab, and she climbed into it and showed him the address on Charlie's phone. She was holding it in her hand.

"Is it far?" she asked the driver in English, and he shook his head.

"No, close. Ten minutes." She nodded and sat stiffly in the seat, trying to make sense of what had just happened. Her marriage was over. She had lost him to another woman and never even noticed, and now they were having a baby. She felt as though she had walked into the middle of the movie. It was a horror movie, one of those films where you wanted to scream and couldn't, like a nightmare, but she couldn't wake up. It was so shocking that she couldn't even cry. She felt like she had just died. Her heart just didn't know it yet, so it was still beating, but the rest of her was dead.

# Chapter 4

Flavia had worn a navy blue wool coat of her own design with a navy cashmere sweater, a simple pencil skirt, and high heels, and carried one of Stella's handbags. She looked chic and serious, as she and Charlie sat in the doctor's waiting room together, waiting to go in. The waiting room was full of pregnant women as Charlie looked around. He felt like he had taken a trip backward in time to twenty years before, when Darcy was pregnant with the twins. But that had been as frightening as it was exciting with all the problems and worries they had to face before the babies were born. This was quiet and calm and easy, and every now and then Flavia smiled at him, and he held her hand.

The technician called him Mr. Tedesco and he didn't correct her. The staff had no way of knowing that he and Flavia weren't married, and Flavia's name was on the forms. She undressed in a little dressing room and came out into the exam room in her underwear and a gown. She lay down on the exam table, and the technician applied the gel to her stomach, just as Charlie remembered, and they waited to watch the screen come alive. It was in color, and seemed easier to decipher on this machine than it had been on the machine of twenty years before. Within seconds, they saw the baby lying inside her, moving and waving an arm as though to say hello. Their eyes filled with tears as they watched it, and Charlie held Flavia's hand again. They saw the heart beating, as the baby moved freely inside her. It was still very small, but was decidedly a baby and seemed already surprisingly well formed. The technician smiled and turned to them.

"Do you want to know the baby's sex?" They said yes in unison, and she pointed. "It's a boy," she said, and Charlie looked shocked at first and then ecstatic. They had been hoping for a girl, but suddenly it didn't matter. They had a son. It was Charlie's first boy. The technician measured the baby from several angles, and confirmed Flavia's due date in August, and then turned off the machine and handed them each a printout of their baby boy. It was a moment they both knew that they would never forget, and even though Charlie had been through it before, it felt new for him all over again. And now he had a son after his two daughters.

Flavia went to dress, and came out looking impeccable and chic again, and they walked out of the room feeling like parents, and closer than ever before. Flavia felt an instant bond to the baby, and another to Charlie. He put an arm around her and kissed her, and they walked out of the office beaming. They were looking at each other, and walked straight ahead toward Flavia's car without seeing the disheveled woman standing right in front of them, in a black coat and black jeans, wearing dark glasses, with a paralyzed look on her face and her heart pounding.

Darcy saw them the moment they walked out the door, and the blind look of ecstasy on their faces. They were only a few feet away from her when Charlie suddenly saw her and stopped in his tracks. The moment he had dreaded for two years had finally come. The greatest joy and the greatest pain within minutes of each other. His eyes filled with tears again, not for himself, but for Darcy and what he had done to her. Her face said it all. Flavia had no idea what had just happened or who Darcy was at first. She didn't recognize her.

"You forgot your phone," Darcy said to Charlie, and handed it to him. When he took it from her he saw that it was his Italian phone, with the text exchange with Flavia about the sonogram still plainly on the screen.

"I'm sorry," he said hoarsely. "We need to talk." And then Flavia realized who she was. She didn't know yet how Darcy had found them, but she had. The two women had met before. They recognized each other now, and Flavia looked at Charlie with fear and deep concern. She didn't know what was about to happen or how Darcy would react.

"I'll see you at the office," Flavia said quietly, with a sad, respectful look at the woman he was still married to. "I'm sorry," she said softly to Darcy, walked to her car, got in, and drove away. It was up to Charlie to deal with Darcy now. She didn't belong in the midst of it, and she felt sorry for Darcy. It was a terrible position for her to be in, one that every woman would dread.

As Darcy stood looking at Charlie, she felt like she was having an out-of-body experience and someone else was speaking. She felt weirdly calm and still in shock, even more so now, looking at him. Instantly they were strangers, not a couple as though a saber had fallen from the sky and severed them from each other.

"I must be incredibly stupid. I never suspected anything, and after I did, it never occurred to me it could be her. I thought you just worked together," Darcy said to him. Flavia was nine years younger than Darcy and they were having a baby. Her own marriage to Charlie was over. It ended when she saw the text message on his phone. They were still standing on the sidewalk. He looked pale and grim. She looked half crazy, but wasn't, just shocked and heartbroken.

"Let's go somewhere to talk," he said quietly. They walked blindly down the street until they came to a little park and sat down on a bench. It had never dawned on her for a minute that her marriage would end on this trip to Rome. But in order for this to happen, it had to have been dead for years. She felt stupid and old and broken, but not even angry yet, only dead and empty.

"How long has it been going on?" she asked him. Long enough to make a baby, although that didn't take long.

"Two years," he said with a somber expression. "I never found the right time to tell you. I should have when it started. I don't know how or why or when, but somehow we let our marriage die. Maybe we were both too busy, or I was, or I traveled too much, or your blog became more important than our marriage. I don't know what happened. And I didn't have the guts to deal with it. I didn't even see it, and by the time I did, it was too late. I was already deeply involved with her by then. This isn't her fault. It's mine."

For the first time, Darcy started to cry, which made it all hurt more. Feeling dead inside was easier. The pain she felt made the loss more real. She had lost him and never even knew it.

"It's partly my fault too. I was so busy with the girls and work, I didn't pay enough attention to you." She realized that now, much,

much too late. "And you're having a baby." He nodded. "When is it due?"

"August."

"Are you going to marry her?" Darcy felt like she was planning her own funeral. But she wanted to know.

"I'd like to. But I didn't want to leave you. It's been confusing, having you both." She could understand now why he didn't want her in Rome. "I love you, Darcy, and I always will, just not in that way anymore." It was the most honest thing he'd said to her in years. His words cut through her like a scalpel, but it was better to know. She appreciated the honesty. She wanted to hate him, but she didn't. She still loved him. She wondered when that would stop.

"Men are lucky, you can start again at any age," she said with an edge to her voice. "Women can't turn the clock back like that, and start having babies again, at fifty or sixty or seventy if they want. It must make you feel young again." She felt ancient at that moment, and as though her life was over. Twenty years down the drain in an instant, when he forgot his phone. It wasn't fair, but she realized she hadn't been fair to him either. There had been times when she had ignored him and taken him for granted. Her job seemed more important than he did.

"I feel young and old," he admitted. "I'm old to be starting over. I hope I don't make the same mistakes again." He sounded sad as he said it.

"At least you're in the same business, maybe that helps," Darcy said, and blew her nose. She couldn't stop crying now. The dam had broken.

"What are you going to tell the girls?" he asked her, and she shook her head. There was no screaming or yelling, no accusations. They were sitting with the dead body of their marriage.

"I have no idea. You'll have to tell them about the baby," Darcy said, and blew her nose again.

"They'll be pissed. I hope they don't hate Flavia for it. This whole mess isn't her fault. It's mine for not telling you two years ago when it started. It was cowardly of me," he readily admitted. Part of him was relieved that she knew now, as hard as it was. At least it was out in the open, and he could stop lying. But he felt like a monster for having hurt her. His and Flavia's momentary joy over the baby was overshadowed by their exposure and Darcy's pain. The look on Darcy's face tore his heart out. "I'm sorry you had to find out like this." She didn't answer for a moment, and nodded, and he recognized the part of Darcy he knew so well, who could handle any crisis and conceal her emotions, just like her parents. It was humiliating to have him see how broken and defeated she felt. She stopped crying and dried her eyes and looked at him coldly. She had run a marathon of emotions in the last hour. The well had run dry. She was drained.

"It had to come out sooner or later. You couldn't keep doing this forever. It must have been complicated." She couldn't even imagine leading a double life as he had—it would have driven her crazy. She was trying to be reasonable and civilized.

"Just so you know, she never asked me to get divorced. She let me handle it the way I wanted, or not handle it. She was perfectly willing to have the baby without being married. She left it up to me."

"That was clever of her," Darcy said darkly. "Maybe if she had asked, you would have run. And now she has the winning card, a baby. I can't compete with that," she said sadly. "That's a powerful force." But she couldn't compete anyway. Their marriage had been dead for too long, and this was the first time she saw it. She hadn't even suspected it before this. Just as he hadn't realized how much they didn't have anymore until he met Flavia and saw the difference, saw what love could still be. "Will you move to Rome?" she asked him. "She can't move to the States, she has a big business here."

"And a big family," he added. "Italian families are different. They stay families forever, they just keep growing, kind of like a tree. They add more branches, and the roots get deeper. It's different in the States. People disperse, they spread out, they move away. They don't hold onto each other the way they do here." She wondered if he was going to abandon the twins now, but she knew how much he loved them.

"You can't run the stores from here, can you?"

"I'd have to do a lot of traveling. We haven't figured that out yet. We didn't have to. I'm here about half the time now." She nodded. It was true, but she had hardly noticed how much he was away. She didn't even miss him when he was gone. She had been blind to all the warning signs for years. She could see that now, and she couldn't entirely blame him for it. She had let it happen too. She stood up then, and looked at him, sitting on the bench. There was so much to decide and figure out. She didn't know where to start. And she wasn't ready to yet. It was all too new and shocking.

"I think we've said enough for now. I have to digest this. I'll go to Paris today. I'll be gone before you come back to the hotel after work. I assume you don't even stay at the hotel when you're here?" She had just figured that out and he didn't answer the question, but it explained the small empty room at the Hassler. He thought she didn't need all the painful details. She knew enough now, and the essence of it. He was in love with another woman, he had cheated on Darcy for two years, and he and the other woman were having a baby. It was more than enough to absorb for one day. They'd have to figure out the rest when they both got home. The house, the girls, where to live, filing for divorce, lawyers. There was so much to think about. "Don't tell Zoe I'm coming to Paris," Darcy said in a devastated voice. "I need a couple of days to myself, without having to put a good face on this for her." She needed to cry her heart out for a few days, and mourn their marriage before they buried it, and announced its death to their daughters. She couldn't imagine what Penny and Zoe would say, except that Penny would forgive him anything, and Zoe would use the divorce and another woman as an excuse to be angry at him, and might blame her mother. Penny wouldn't blame either of them. It wasn't in her nature. She would be compassionate and supportive. Zoe would take it personally.

Charlie got up from the bench and walked along beside Darcy for a few minutes without saying anything. She had run out of words and feelings. She felt like she had none left for anyone, not even for herself. She didn't know what she felt for him. Contempt, anger, hurt, pity, disappointment, rage, fear of the future. It all washed over her like a tidal wave. She left him a few minutes later and walked back to the hotel alone. It had been the worst day of her life.

When Darcy walked into Charlie's hotel room, she sat down on the bed and stared into space, seeing only the deep black hole her life had fallen into. It looked like a bottomless abyss. She saw the sheets on the unmade bed they had slept in hours before and realized that it had been the last night she would ever spend with him, and suddenly she started to cry and couldn't stop. He was more than just her husband, he was her family and best friend. They would always be connected because of their children, but her life with him was over. She couldn't run away from it. She wondered what would have happened if she hadn't read the text that morning when she found his phone after he left. How long would he have kept up the charade? He would have gotten caught sooner or later, and it was hard to believe he had managed to keep it from her for two years. It was a sharp reminder to her that she hadn't been paying attention to him or their marriage.

She didn't hate Flavia for it, or even him. There was no one to hate, not even herself. She wished they had done better at keeping their relationship strong. It had gotten away from her when she wasn't looking. She thought he would be there forever, and it felt now like he had died, or she had. This felt worse than losing her parents, because they had both been older and not in good health, and her father couldn't survive without her mother. She wondered suddenly if she could survive without Charlie and felt a wave of panic wash over her. It wasn't supposed to end this way. She had expected Charlie to be with her for many, many more years, forever, and now he was gone, suddenly, with no warning. He belonged to someone else. It seemed unspeakably cruel.

And it was deeply upsetting that he might be living in Italy, and not in the States. He wouldn't be there to help her. She wondered how the twins would feel about that, or about any of it. He had a new woman in his life, and in six months a baby. There'd been no warning for the twins either. The news of their parents' divorce was going to fall out of the sky and hit them like a meteor. She had no idea when Charlie would want to tell them, or what he would say. They were old enough to be told most of it. She thought the details should come from their father, since he had made the mess by jumping the gun with Flavia and the baby, if he had wanted a divorce. He said he hadn't wanted that before he met her, but Darcy wondered now if he was telling the truth or had wanted out before Flavia. When did he stop loving Darcy, or did it matter now?

She tidied up the mess in her suitcase, with a DO NOT DISTURB sign on the door so no one would come in and see her crying. She couldn't stop. She wasn't angry. She was overwhelmingly sad.

She ordered a cup of tea. She hadn't eaten all day, but she wasn't hungry, and didn't care. Her breakfast hadn't arrived before she left the hotel. When she turned on the TV just to hear a voice in the room, she was startled to hear a report on the new virus that she had heard a rumor about recently in New York. They were calling it Co 2-24.

The news team reported random cases that had cropped up in different areas of Asia, and that their origins could not be traced so far. They also said that this virus was considered far less dangerous than Covid-19 had been, and that another pandemic was not expected. But the new cases reported in Europe, and several in the U.S., had caught scientists' attention, and they were studying it now. They emphasized that there was no cause for panic, but the new virus was worthy of the public's attention, and they recommended the same cautions that had been used four years before: social distancing, frequent hand washing, and masks in public places frequented by large crowds. Beyond that, no directives had been issued, or recommended.

They confirmed that the Covid-19 vaccine did not appear to protect the public from Co 2-24. The symptoms were similar, though it was not as extreme or thought to be as lethal, but the outbreaks suggested a high level of contagion in certain segments of the population, mainly the elderly and people with other health issues like cancer or heart disease. It had not yet been detected in children, but adolescents were at high risk with a high degree of socialization among them and little caution to protect themselves. The report sounded alarmist to Darcy after a few minutes and she turned off the TV. Her marriage had just died. She didn't need to hear about another virus to terrorize her. There had been numerous scares in the past four years, all of them unfounded. Whenever the news ran thin, they came up with another virus story. Darcy had enough real drama on her plate at the moment.

The concierge got her a six P.M. flight to Paris. She had to leave for the airport at four. She put on a black sweater with her black jeans, nicer shoes, and brushed her hair into a bun for the flight. She didn't bother with makeup. Charlie texted her halfway through the afternoon, with a message that only made things worse.

"I'm sorry, Darcy. I know it's hard to believe, but I love you. I always will. I'm sorry for the disruption and heartbreak now, but in the end I think we'll both have better lives after this." It made her want to throw her phone at the wall. He was going to have a better life with an instant new wife and a baby. What did she have? Nothing. Two daughters who had already flown the nest, and a husband who had been cheating on her for two years and no longer wanted her.

She felt like her life was over at forty-two. She couldn't imagine finding another man to love, or wanting to. Life with Charlie hadn't been perfect, but it had been good enough. She thought they were happy but apparently she was wrong.

The bellman picked up her bags at three-thirty. She was wearing dark glasses to hide her swollen eyes.

She had called the Hotel Belle Ville in the 7th arrondissement on the Left Bank in Paris. She and Charlie always stayed there. It was small and charming, in a beautiful old house. There were twelve rooms. The staff served breakfast in the morning, consisting of pastries and delicious coffee, in the lobby, in big comfortable chairs. She and Charlie had been staying there for twenty years, and they preferred it to all the five-star palaces. It was going to be a good place to hide and lick her wounds for a few days, and then see Zoe when she was ready. They had time. She felt as though she had been in a serious accident.

She thought about everything that had happened and that she had discovered as she was about to leave the Hassler, and one of the things she found so upsetting, as she looked back over the landscape of the past two years and thought of all the things she had done with Charlie—the trips they'd gone on, the events they'd attended, the family gatherings for holidays with Zoe and Penny, a few romantic weekends here and there, their relaxing weekends in the Hamptons with and without the girls, the friends they'd had dinner with—was that all the while he had a whole second life going on with Flavia, with special moments with her too. It made their last two years together feel like a total hoax he had perpetrated on her. Was it all fake, or just some of it? Was he pretending to care about her and didn't? She no longer trusted a single moment they'd spent together or anything he'd said. She couldn't imagine trusting him or any other man ever again. The joke had been on her, while his heart and mind were in Rome the entire time. Throughout history, for centuries, men had had second families, hidden away in the next town in horse-and-buggy days and Victorian times, or in other countries in modern times with jet travel as Charlie had done. The game the men played was as old as the ages, and one day the two women and two families would find out about each other, with a brood of children in both homes, and all hell would break loose. That was exactly where Darcy was now. There wasn't even anything different or creative about it. It was actually very mundane, except to her it was anything but mundane. It was profoundly shocking, and it was the long-term duplicity she found so hard to swallow and kept running through her mind again and again. It told her that she really didn't know Charlie, or what kind of man he was. But he certainly wasn't the upstanding husband she always thought him. He was just another cheater and liar, with a woman and a second family in another city. As she walked out of his hotel room, the anger she hadn't felt until then rose up in her throat like bile, and nearly choked her. In a single day he had turned her love for him to ash. There was nothing left of her or their marriage.

When Charlie got back to the office after he left Darcy, he called Flavia in hers to see if she was free. She had just gotten out of a finance meeting to go over the budget for the fashion week show in Milan. They were only slightly over budget this time, which was a vast improvement over last time. Just creating the samples for the runway cost a fortune, as did the models they hired, and the elaborate décor by a stage set designer. But it was worth the investment to showcase the collection.

"Can I come up?" Charlie asked her when she answered her phone. He sounded solemn, and she was still shaken too by the scene with Darcy outside the doctor's office. The exciting news that they were having a baby boy was eclipsed for the moment by the drama that had unfolded. Charlie was in her office less than five minutes later. He looked like he had been dropped out of an airplane without a parachute. It had been one of the worst moments of his life, facing Darcy and the look in her eyes of total betrayal by the person she trusted and loved most. He knew he'd never forget it. Nor would she.

He sat down across from Flavia and melted into the chair as though his bones had dissolved, along with his heart. In contrast was the excitement over their baby boy.

"What happened after I left?" Flavia asked him quietly. "Did she make a terrible scene?" It was what she had imagined would happen when Charlie and Darcy were alone.

"Not at all. That's not her style. She has too much dignity to do that. Usually, she's good at covering her emotions. But I broke her heart. I could see it in her eyes. Your brother was right. I should have done it a long time ago. I didn't have the guts," he said humbly. "Thank you for letting me do it at my own pace, even if I was wrong." He knew that now.

"You're lucky she's not Italian. An Italian woman would have made a scene, screamed and yelled, torn out her hair and yours, and maybe stabbed you." She smiled a small cautious smile at him, and he laughed in spite of himself. She could always lighten the moment and make him feel better.

"At least I know what to expect if I ever screw up with you." But he couldn't imagine Flavia behaving that way either. They were both noble women who wouldn't make a scene. He was lucky in that regard. It almost made him feel worse that Darcy was so civil about it.

"What are you going to do now, or what will she?" Flavia felt deeply sorry for Darcy. It was every woman's worst nightmare. Flavia had thought of her often, but Darcy had never been real to her, until she stood facing her that morning. And now she was very real.

"She's leaving for Paris tonight and going back to New York after fashion week. I'm going back the week before. I'll get my lawyers to start working on the financial settlement. I want to be generous with her. It doesn't make up for what I did, but I don't want anything to change in her life. I'm going to give her the house in the city and the house in the Hamptons, everything in both houses, all the art, a settlement, and spousal support. She won't have any financial worries." He could afford it, and he wanted to start fresh with Flavia, without souvenirs from the past. "I have to check, but I think we can be divorced in six months. We might even be able to get married right before the baby . . . our son . . . is born." He smiled sadly and reached for her hand, and she held his tightly.

"I'm sorry this happened today," she said softly.

"So am I, but it had to happen." The baby had become more real to him today too. It wasn't just a romantic notion, or an imaginary bond. It was a real flesh-and-blood human being, another family he was starting, with all the responsibilities that went with it. At fifty-two, he was starting over again.

They talked quietly for a while, and then he went back to his of-fice. There was so much to think about now. And when he reached into his pocket for something, he found the small printout from the sonogram. He sat looking at it for a long time, trying not to think of Darcy, and focusing only on Flavia and their baby boy. He wondered what he'd look like, what kind of man he would become one day. He hoped that he'd be more like Flavia than himself. He wasn't proud of what had been revealed that day. He wanted to be a better man, a better human being, a better husband than the one who had hurt Darcy so badly. He knew that she might forgive him one day, but it would be a long time before he'd forgive himself. And he hoped that one day he would be worthy of Flavia's faith in him, and love. He had a long way to go.

# Chapter 5

The Hotel Belle Ville on the rue Bonaparte was always as beautiful as Darcy remembered it. It was like a little jewel box, with beautiful rooms filled with antiques. The staff maintained it perfectly and Darcy considered it one of the best-kept secrets in Paris. She and Charlie had spent some wonderful vacations there, which she didn't want to think about now. She could have gone to a more impersonal larger hotel like the Ritz or the George V or the Crillon, but she felt so battered that she wanted to be somewhere smaller and familiar, where she could lick her wounds and hide. Being at the Belle Ville was like a warm embrace in elegant surroundings. She always felt like Marie Antoinette when she stayed there. It was like a tiny corner of Versailles with exquisite furniture and art. The rates were high, but worth every euro they charged. It was one of the best-kept secrets in Paris, with an exclusive clientele.

It was gray and rainy the night she arrived from Rome, which seemed appropriate, and the next day as well. Her heart felt beaten to a pulp and she stayed in bed and slept all day. She took a sleeping pill she kept for emergencies that night, so she didn't wake up in the middle of the night and think about what had happened. She didn't want to think about Charlie or Flavia or their baby, or even her own children. She had sustained a deep wound, like a serious accident. She needed time to heal, at least enough so that she could function, see Zoe, and figure out what to do next. And she didn't want to tell Zoe yet about the divorce. And when she did, she would have to tell Penny too. She couldn't handle that yet.

On her second day in Paris, she woke up in time for breakfast if she wanted it. She was still groggy from the sleeping pill she'd taken, but a cappuccino sounded heavenly, and she could smell the aromas of coffee and fresh pastry wafting up from downstairs. She had eaten nothing the day before. She finally decided to get up, put on an old pair of jeans, a black sweater, and ballet shoes, pulled her hair into a ponytail, and headed downstairs. She felt fragile, as though all the bones in her body had been broken, or gotten a tremendous shaking. But the world around her looked normal. Half a dozen guests were drinking coffee and eating croissants, and brioche filled with chocolate, sitting in the big comfortable chairs.

She helped herself to a cappuccino and a croissant, found an empty chair, and looked out into the garden. It was a sunny day, and she glanced at the guests. Two older ladies who were speaking German, a young couple who looked like honeymooners, speaking Spanish, an English couple looking as if they were going to walk over the moors in tweeds, and a tall, very erect man somewhere in his forties with almost military bearing, a chiseled face, salt-and-pepper hair and electric blue eyes, in a black sweater and jeans. She noticed him almost mechanically and guessed he was American, but she didn't hear him speak to anyone. He was alone. He had copies of the London *Financial Times* and *The Wall Street Journal* and some papers under his arm. He sat down in a chair not too far from Darcy, read the papers, and made some notes on a yellow pad. He looked busy, and he glanced over and saw her staring into space with a tragic expression, then went back to his yellow pad. She paid no attention to him. He left a short while later and she went back upstairs to her room and decided to go for a walk. She didn't want to run into Zoe— it was Saturday, and she might be out and about.

Darcy put on the peacoat she'd brought, and running shoes, and a little while later she left the hotel and walked across the bridge to the Right Bank, to the Tuileries Gardens near the Louvre. She stopped along the way and looked at the boats on the Seine from the bridge. Everyone seemed busy, and the city was alive. It was chilly, but she felt better after she'd walked for an hour. The hangover from the sleeping pill had worn off by then.

She sat on a bench in the Tuileries, trying to fit the puzzle pieces of her life together, and make sense of what had happened in Rome. It didn't make sense at all to her, and it wasn't fair. Charlie had snuck out and built a whole new life without warning her that their house was on fire, and by the time he told her, it had burned to the ground. Now she had to piece her own life back together from the ashes. Things weren't supposed to work out this way. Why were Flavia and Charlie the lucky winners and she was now all alone? It made her feel vulnerable and small, the way she had when her parents died. But she hadn't been heartbroken, and she had had Charlie then, to lean on and to protect her. Now she had no one. She had to pretend to be strong for her daughters when she told them what had happened and that she and Charlie were getting a divorce. She was thinking about calling Zoe the next day, if she felt up to seeing her. She had to be strong for them. It was the weekend, and Zoe wouldn't be in class. Darcy had thought she and Charlie would be somewhere in Italy for a romantic weekend. Instead she was alone in Paris, nursing a broken heart, and trying to find the pieces of her life in the rubble. She felt as though she'd been beaten or shot.

She walked back to the hotel and saw the man she thought was American on his way out. They almost collided with each other, and she nearly tripped trying to avoid him. He reached out quickly and grabbed her arm to steady her before she fell. He had a powerful grip and warm eyes with lines in the corners when he smiled.

"I'm sorry," she said in a muffled voice, and didn't smile back. She couldn't.

"I bumped into you," he reminded her, and she heard that she'd been right. He was American. She wasn't sure if his slight drawl was from Texas or the South. He had an old black leather jacket over his arm, and was carrying a briefcase. He didn't look like a businessman, but he had a serious, purposeful look, as though he had things to do. She tried to guess what line of work he might be in, but she couldn't, and an instant later, he hurried out and hailed a cab near the hotel. Darcy went back to her room and took a nap, and when she woke up that afternoon, she sent Zoe a text to call her when she had time. She thought she could handle seeing her, and she wanted to. It would be comforting even if Zoe didn't know what had happened. And she didn't want to miss out on time with her.

It was after eight that night when Zoe called. Darcy was thinking about dinner. She hadn't eaten since breakfast. She hadn't been hungry in two days. There was a good bistro down the street from the hotel, but it seemed like a big effort to go out. She was exhausted from everything she'd been through. But she had always been able to appear calm in a crisis.

"Hi, Mom, how are you?" Zoe's bouncy, energetic voice came on the line, and Darcy smiled, until she remembered the news she had to tell her, but not yet.

"I'm fine. What are you up to?" Darcy tried to sound as normal as she could, so Zoe didn't guess anything was amiss. She doubted that Charlie would have told her anything yet. He needed time to figure out what to say. How and when he told the twins was going to be important.

"Jean-Paul and I were thinking about dinner. Are you in the Hamptons or New York?" Darcy hesitated for a fraction of a second, and forced herself to sound upbeat for her daughter. It took all the strength she had.

"Neither one. Guess where I am?"

"L.A.?" Darcy went to movie industry events frequently for her blog. She had been to the Grammys recently. She had taken the girls a few times.

"Nope. Paris. I got here tonight." It was a lie but a small one and did no harm.

"You're here early," Zoe sounded surprised.

"I stopped in Rome to visit Dad. He has a busy week, so I thought I'd come to see you. I've got some appointments here next week, and

I thought we could have some time together before everything gets nuts for fashion week." No one could have guessed how ravaged she felt. She covered the damage well.

"You're not going to Milan?" Zoe asked her, as Jean-Paul teased her and kissed her neck, and Zoe laughed. He distracted her enough that she didn't pay close attention to her mother's voice and had no reason to suspect a problem.

"Paris is enough. I don't need to do Milan too. I'd rather spend time with you. Do you have a busy week next week?"

"Not too bad," Zoe said casually, smiling at Jean-Paul. He was a handsome young man with dark hair and deep brown eyes. He was tall and thin and didn't have the obsession with bodybuilding of American men his age. At twenty-six, he was almost a full-fledged doctor. He wanted to be a cardiac surgeon but had several more years to study. His father was an orthopedic surgeon and his mother was an oncologist, both respected professors at the Faculté de Méde-cine, where he was studying. "How's Dad?" Zoe asked, since Darcy had said she'd seen him.

"Crazy busy, getting ready for fashion week in Milan," and a new baby, she didn't add. Darcy had an idea then. "Do you want to have dinner with me tonight? I was thinking about going to the bistro down the street. It's pretty good." Hearing Zoe's voice, she was eager to see her.

Zoe conferred quickly with Jean-Paul, who nodded enthusiasti-cally. He was starving and had just come home from his last class. "Sure."

"Meet you there in twenty minutes?" Darcy suggested, and they agreed. She brushed her hair and put on lipstick. She looked beaten up, but she could attribute it to travel fatigue if Zoe noticed, but she didn't.

Half an hour later, they were sitting at the bistro. Darcy ordered chicken, and Zoe and Jean-Paul ordered steak and the thin crispy French fries that they both loved.

Darcy gave her daughter a big hug when they arrived at the restaurant, and Jean-Paul politely shook her hand. He was as pleasant and good-looking as Darcy remembered him from their earlier meeting. He was well brought up and intelligent, and he and Zoe were crazy about each other. Their youthful excitement reminded Darcy of how she had felt about Charlie when she met him while she was in college. The memory cut through her like a knife, and she forced her mind back to the present.

It boosted Darcy's spirits to see her daughter. Zoe didn't suspect anything unusual about her mother's appearance or her spirits. Seeing Zoe made her happy, so it was easier to conceal the effect of the shock she'd had in Rome. And being with her was part of the healing process.

They made plans for the week while they were at dinner, and shared a bottle of wine. There was a festive mood at the table. Zoe was visibly happy to see her mother. She hadn't seen her since New Year when she went back to Paris after Christmas. She was loving Paris, Jean-Paul, and her studies at the Sorbonne. They were both serious students, and Jean-Paul was at the hospital every day, observing surgeries and assisting with patients. Darcy asked him about it, and she was impressed yet again with how dedicated he was to the field of medicine. He said he had always wanted to be a doctor since both his parents were. He had years ahead of him to train for his specialty, and Darcy loved how respectful he was of Zoe. He had good values and said he was close to his parents. They loved to travel together, and he had been to Africa, India, and Asia with them. He was a well-rounded person for his age, and Darcy could see how in love with him Zoe was, although she was seven years younger than Jean-Paul.

"They've been lending me to other departments in the hospital lately. There's been a terrible flu epidemic for the past month," he said matter-of-factly.

"Not Covid-19, I hope," Darcy said.

"No, a lot of it is this new Co 2-24 that's related to it but not as bad, though people still get pretty sick. It causes heart complications so I've been helping in Cardiac ICU, with full protection of course. It responds to some traditional medications, and they're going to start working on a vaccine for it now. A few older people have died from it, and one young girl last week, but she was a transplant patient, so she was more vulnerable."

"I've heard some talk of it," Darcy said, "and something on CNN in Rome the other day. I hope we're not heading for another pandemic."

"I don't think so," Jean-Paul said seriously, "although I don't know a lot about it. I'm not important enough to be in the senior staff meetings. But if there were any risk of that, the government would shut us down and confine everyone much faster this time. And we'd be much better prepared than last time. The World Pandemic Organization supervises supplies in every country. Last time, no one had ever experienced anything like it before. But they say that Co 2-24 is much less dangerous than Covid-19 was."

"I hope they're right."

Zoe and Jean-Paul walked Darcy back to her hotel after dinner, and then walked the rest of the way home. It had been a nice evening with her mother, and Jean-Paul liked her too. Darcy was thinking about them when she went back to her room. Young love was so innocent, they had their whole lives ahead of them to do whatever they wanted and follow their dreams. Jean-Paul's were very clear, and for her age, Zoe's were too. They were sweet together, but just looking at them was bittersweet for Darcy. They had all of life's wonderful surprises ahead of them, babies, and loves, and exciting people they'd meet, and bitter disappointments too. She was relieved that Zoe hadn't noticed her mother's somber mood. She had covered it well, or so she thought.

Penny called Zoe that night to check on her. She mentioned that there was a minor flu epidemic in Hong Kong too, but she and her roommates were being careful and none of them were sick.

"How's Mom?" she asked her sister when Zoe told her that Darcy was in Paris.

"I don't know. She seemed okay, but something was weird. She acted normal, but her eyes were sad, especially when I asked how Dad was when she saw him."

"She's probably just tired from the trip, or disappointed that he didn't have time to go away somewhere with her. You know how he gets when he's traveling. He has a million appointments, and no time for her."

"Maybe. I just thought she was a little off. Have you met any cute boys yet?" That was of greater interest to Zoe.

"We met some last week, but they're kind of geeks. But we're going to a party this weekend. One of our neighbors is giving a barbecue on the roof." Penny lived in a fun building with lots of young people, whose parents had rented them luxurious apartments. And they had a rooftop garden, a pool, and a gym.

They talked for a few minutes and hung up, and Zoe forgot about her mother being "weird" when she and Jean-Paul went to bed. They were looking forward to Sunday with no classes, although they both had lots of homework, and they had promised to have lunch with Zoe's mother on Monday. It was going to be a nice week.

Darcy kept busy for the next few days, taking photographs and diligently doing research for her blog, to distract herself from everything that had happened. Her discoveries in Rome almost seemed unreal. She was going to take her wedding ring off but she was afraid Zoe would notice it. She had a long list of places to check out for her blog, and forced herself to go to most of them and wrote the text to go with the photos. She had an easy writing style which her readers enjoyed. Several publishers had asked her to consider writing a book based on her blog, and her life as an influencer. She was an icon in the world of social media, but for the moment she was content to write her blog and didn't feel ready for a bigger project like a book. Especially now, she felt as though someone had let the air out of her tires in Rome. She couldn't believe how exhausted she was, it really felt like she'd had an accident, and both her mind and body were still in shock. She had to force herself to get moving every day, and keep going. She did it with sheer grit. She was a strong, disciplined person and she wasn't going to let what Charlie had done destroy her. She was determined to survive it and come out whole at the other end, but it wasn't easy.

She lay awake all night every night, thinking of all the times she realized now that he had lied to her. There were too many to count now that she knew the whole story. She hadn't heard from Charlie again after she left Rome, which was just as well, but it hurt anyway. She had to get used to the idea that nothing was ever going to be the same again. Everything would change and she had to change with it. She had never expected to find herself alone after twenty years of marriage. She had spent half her life with him. And most of her identity, except for the blog, was entangled in the role of being his wife, which left her wondering who she was now. She was no longer sure. A blogger, an influencer, and a mother, but what else? She had no idea. But she wasn't going to let him crush her identity or destroy her. She had to protect herself. She felt like she had run into a wall every time she realized she had lost him. He was already gone and had been for two years. She just didn't know it then, but now she did.

Flavia was very busy getting ready for fashion week, the following week in Milan. Her collection was ready. The final fittings with the models got done, the music had been chosen, the sets were being built. They had taken the entire collection to Milan in a truck two days before the show. Milan was always chaotic the week before fashion week, and even more so the actual week of all the runway shows. The press was there from all over the world, and designers went crazy correcting final details and anything that went wrong or needed changing at the last minute. Some model they were counting on always got sick or canceled, and they had to search frantically to replace her. Everyone was already booked to walk the shows, so they often had to fly in a new model from New York. There were a million small and big things that could go wrong, and the miraculous sewers worked night and day until the last second, right before the models came down the runway with sixty to a hundred looks, depending on the designer.

Considering how insane it usually got, Charlie was always impressed by how calm Flavia appeared. He knew she wasn't, but she looked that way, and handled every crisis with poise as it came.

Charlie stopped in to see Roberto at the Tedesco office in Milan. He looked harassed. Stella and Bianca were there. Their show was the next day, and the women went off to check the lineup of accessories again. Roberto gave Charlie a knowing look after they left.

"I hear you had an interesting encounter after the doctor a week ago," he said, and Charlie knew instantly what he meant.

"It was my worst nightmare come true, but it had to happen sooner or later. It was just very unfortunate." Charlie looked sad as he said it, thinking about Darcy. "She's a good person and deserved better."

"At least you'll be free now," Roberto said quietly. "Are you coming to our show?"

"Of course. And Flavia's is the day after. Are you going to hers?" Charlie asked him. Roberto laughed at the question.

"In full force, we're all going. I wouldn't miss it." They were loyal to each other. They never let each other down. Flavia was going to theirs with him the next day. They all sat together, the whole Tedesco clan. They were a major force, with Umberto as the king who ruled his kingdom with Francesca at his side, all of them looking devastatingly chic as photographers rushed to photograph them.

Predictably, the Tedesco show was a big success, it always was. They were the mainstay of Italian fashion. Theirs weren't daring and high fashion the way Flavia's designs were, but Tedesco was a brand stores could rely on for big sales with all their high-end clients.

And the day after, Flavia's show was a major hit. The reviews were fabulous, and they said it was her best show in her three years in business. She was now at the forefront of fashion in Italy. She had made her mark with her brand, and it was exciting to see the models pound down the runway in each creation more exciting than the last one. The show was exceptionally beautiful, as were the models who wore the clothes. Charlie was proud of her as he watched it, and went backstage to congratulate her when it was over. She looked exhausted but delighted, and had taken her bow at the end of the show.

There was a cocktail reception afterward for important editors and media, and a dinner after that. Flavia wore one of the runway samples. It fit her perfectly. The baby didn't show yet.

Charlie was circulating in the crowd at the cocktail party, greeting people he knew, and heard several times in the conversations around him that a number of people in the fashion world had gotten sick recently, and a few of them had been admitted to hospitals. The editor of *British Vogue* mentioned that her father-in-law was very sick with complications from a virus that had stricken him two weeks ago. It seemed to be a recurring theme as Charlie made his way around the room, and he said something about it to Roberto when he saw him at the dinner for Flavia's brand.

"Are you hearing the talk about people getting sick with a new virus?" Charlie asked him.

"Some. They say it's just an ordinary flu, nothing to worry about. I know a few people in Rome who had it. It's not Covid-19 again. That won't happen. We've all been vaccinated."

"People are saying that this could be dangerous too, that it's not as serious but there's no vaccine for it." Charlie didn't like what he was hearing, and he was particularly disturbed for Flavia's sake since she was pregnant. Roberto seemed certain that the media were playing it up to be sensational, and prey on people's fears, which seemed irresponsible to Charlie if it were true.

They left the dinner party after midnight, and Flavia couldn't wait to go to their hotel and get to bed. She had worked through the night on final adjustments and fittings for the past week. Fashion week was always brutally hard work for everyone involved, including the designer. She was sound asleep in bed before he got his clothes off. But all the hard work paid off when they saw her reviews in the morning papers. It was one of those sweet moments of victory that he loved sharing with her. They had breakfast together, reading all the papers and savoring her success before they went back to Rome that afternoon.

"Do you want to go to Paris for the shows next week?" she asked him with a hopeful look, but he shook his head.

"I want to be in Rome to make sure all our orders get placed, and to see what my buyers are ordering. And Darcy's in Paris. She's at every show and I don't want to run into her right now. It's all a little

too fresh." Flavia nodded. It made sense. "And I don't like what I'm hearing about this virus that's floating around Europe. I've heard about it from England now too. Several people have mentioned people who've caught it in Italy, and the editor of *Vogue Germany* said her husband just got out the hospital with it. It attacks the heart instead of the lungs, and can cause heart attacks in severe cases. I don't think you should expose yourself right now. You should ask your doctor about it."

"I think people are panicking over nothing, because of what happened with Covid-19. Everyone says this is much milder, like an ordinary flu."

"A lot of people seem to be getting it." Charlie disagreed with her. "And it's no joke if it causes heart complications. I'd rather stay in Italy with you than wander around Europe right now. And I need to be here for work anyway for the next week or so, and then I need to get back to New York to see my lawyers." He wanted to get the divorce started so he could marry Flavia before she had the baby, and now Darcy knew, so he wanted to move quickly. Flavia had a week off after the show, before starting work on her next collection. It was one of the few times she ever slowed down, after her runway show during fashion week. She was happy to have him at home in Rome with her. They could be open about their relationship now, which made them both feel more relaxed, and she had told her father about the baby and Charlie's imminent divorce after their show. He said he was very happy and had congratulated them both. The timing of her announcement had been perfect.

*　*　*

Despite the heartbreak Darcy was concealing from her daughter, she and Zoe enjoyed each other's company, and it was a healing, loving touch on Darcy's grief during the week leading up to fashion week in Paris. They went to several museums together, had lunches in their favorite restaurants, and did some shopping, all the things they loved doing together. Their time was especially meaningful to Darcy, knowing that hard times lay ahead when she went home, which made her feel closer to her daughter.

Zoe said she was sorry her father wasn't with them, and Darcy didn't say a word when she said it, which Zoe found odd. It happened again, and Zoe called Penny in Hong Kong, to share her concerns.

"Something weird *is* going on," Zoe insisted. "Mom hasn't said a word about Dad all week. If I mention him, she looks stone-faced and doesn't comment. They must have had a fight in Rome or something."

"You're being dramatic. They're probably both just busy and tired. I spoke to Dad two days ago, and he sounds fine. He's been to all the big shows in Milan, and he said the season is looking great. He's going to order a ton of things for the store."

"Mom says she hasn't talked to him since she's been here. I'm telling you, something odd is going on," Zoe insisted, and Penny assured her again that she was wrong.

But something even odder happened the next day. Paris Fashion Week was due to start in three days, but a notice appeared in all the French newspapers. Due to a new virus that had begun to crop up all over Europe, in order to avoid a worldwide crisis like the one four years before with Covid-19, the French government was canceling fashion week by governmental order, all nonessential stores and business were ordered to close, and people were being confined to their homes and would have to work remotely for the next three weeks, or until further notice. The authorities weren't waiting to see what happened this time. The government moved fast, and urged people to return to their home cities and countries in the next twenty-four hours if they wished to do so. After that the borders of France would be closed and no one could enter or leave the country.

The announcement set off a wave of panic all over Paris, and Darcy called Zoe to tell her as soon as she heard that fashion week had been canceled. Millions of dollars already spent on the shows would be lost, but the government preferred the loss to the economy rather than risk an epidemic that could get out of hand like the last one. They wanted to stop the virus immediately this time and limit the opportunities for contagion. Masks were required everywhere.

The Sorbonne closed the same day, with instructions to follow classes online. Systems that had been used the last time were imple-mented again. Darcy met Zoe at her apartment an hour later, and Jean-Paul joined them soon after. He was going to stay with Zoe for the three-week confinement since he slept there every night anyway, except when he was on duty at the hospital as part of his training.

"My parents think this could be as bad as the last one," he told them with a solemn expression. And since they were both doctors, Darcy believed him.

"Are you going back to New York, Mom?" Zoe asked her, looking frightened.

"I don't really have anything to go back to. You're here, Penny's in Hong Kong. Your father's in Italy. I don't know what his plans are. You and I could go home, I suppose. Do you want to?"

"I want to stay here with Jean-Paul," Zoe said in a soft voice, not sure what her mother would say.

"Then I'll stay here too," Darcy said decisively. "I can stay at the hotel," since there was no room for her in Zoe's tiny apartment, especially if Jean-Paul would be staying with her in the only bed. The hotel was more comfortable for Darcy since she had a suite.

"Shouldn't we call Dad and ask what he's doing if they lock down in Italy too?" The news was already all over Europe that France was confining their citizens, and Germany and Spain said they were too, and closing their borders. It was all frighteningly reminiscent of Covid-19, but what all the governments wanted was to avoid allowing a new virus epidemic to reach the same proportions. These were early measures to stop the virus before it became a pandemic and blazed out of control.

"I have a feeling your father will stay in Italy," Darcy said quietly. It was obvious to her because of Flavia, but she didn't want to say anything about that to Zoe, since the twins knew nothing about it yet, or that they were getting a divorce. Darcy wanted them both home when she and Charlie told them, so they'd have both their parents' presence and support, which meant June, when the girls came home to New York.

Zoe called her father, and he confirmed what her mother had said. Italy had just announced their own lockdown, and he said it was simpler for him to stay where he was.

"Do you want to come to Paris, Dad?" she asked him innocently.

"You can stay with Mom at the hotel. Jean-Paul is going to stay at my place with me."

"It's going to be chaos trying to get from one place to another right now. The Italians are clamping down immediately because it got so bad last time. I'm fine in Rome at the hotel. And it's good that your mother is in Paris with you." Zoe tried not to read anything into what he said. It all made sense. They called Penny two hours later, and Hong Kong was shutting down too. Penny said she'd be fine in the apartment with her roommates. Hong Kong was locking down for a month, and she said they had plenty to do, and would follow their classes online, as Zoe and Jean-Paul were going to do in Paris, and students all over Europe.

By midnight in Paris, six P.M. in New York, the United States had shut down too. Borders were closed all over the world. Planes were going to be grounded except for the next twenty-four hours so people could return to their homes.

The entire world was grinding to a halt, just as it had four years before, but all on the same day this time, and long before Co 2-24 could become a pandemic. They were going to beat it this time by all the means they had learned before—confinement, quarantine, social distancing, systematically shutting every country down and isolating them. They had all been there before. And this time each government wanted to win the battle without sustaining the shocking loss of life they had experienced before, and without the crippling blow to economies from having to shut them down for so long. Government leaders said it was going to be a fast battle this time and the virus was going to die, not their citizens. People were told to wear gloves and masks if they went outdoors and to do so as seldom as possible, and only for the most vital needs—food, or visits to doctors, hospitals, or pharmacies. Hospitals were not allowing visits again. No other reasons for leaving home would be allowed.

Italy had opted for a four-week confinement too, and Flavia looked at Charlie in shock.

"I can't believe we have to go through this again," she said. "Thank goodness it's happening after the show."

"I don't want you going anywhere," he told her sternly. "You have to protect yourself and the baby."

"I'm glad you'll be here with me," she said, and put her arms around him and kissed him.

"Is that allowed?" Charlie asked her, worried.

"It's obligatory," she said, as they watched the news. Country after country announced their quarantines. In a way, it was a relief, knowing that governments had reacted quickly this time. It was going to be a long, very quiet three or four weeks. But they had all done it before, and they would get through it again. And this time, Flavia and Charlie would be together.

# Chapter 6

When Darcy left Zoe at her apartment with Jean-Paul, and went back to the Hotel Belle Ville, she saw a small group of people gathered around the front desk, with the manager explaining to them that they had to leave by morning. The hotel was closing. The management had to release their employees to confine themselves at home. They had been closed for four months during the pandemic, and they hoped that this time the shutdown would be much shorter, if the government succeeded in beating the new virus quickly. But for the moment, all guests had to leave, find other lodgings, or return to their own homes. The manager further informed them that the five-star hotels were also closing. He said that a few small hotels were remaining open, but he had no idea which they were. Darcy listened from a short distance away and waited until all but one of the other guests had gone to their rooms to pack. The concierge was making plane reservations for them to leave on the last planes out of France, before the airport closed by noon the next day. This shutdown was far more radical than the previous one had been, but hopefully more effective and would last for a much shorter time.

The other guest remaining at the desk, the American man whom Darcy had seen before, signaled to her to go first. She stepped closer to the desk to explain her situation to the manager.

"I have a daughter studying in Paris, at the Sorbonne. She's living in a tiny apartment, and staying here for the confinement, and I need to be in Paris with her, but I can't stay at her apartment. I need a place to go to. It can be very simple, but I need somewhere to stay. Do you have any idea which hotels might be open?"

"To be honest, madame, none that I know of. It's just too complicated for most small hotels, and the big ones are closing too." He looked apologetic but was at a loss as to what to suggest. He hesitated for a moment as the man next to her expressed the same problem.

"I'm just back from Saudi Arabia, after finishing an assignment there. I'm waiting for my next mission, and my employer needs me to stay here. I'm an engineer and could be sent anywhere to help with a national emergency. This happened so rapidly, I'm really stuck." The manager looked from one to the other with dismay, and then had an idea.

"I might know of a possibility. It's a rather unusual Airbnb. It's a private home. The woman who owns it has two rooms to rent. She did so last time, but she's quite old, and it's been four years. I have no idea if she's still operating. She was a famous actress a long time ago. She's retired and she has a beautiful house, and her two guest suites are exceptional, but she must be eighty-five or -six by now. You may have heard of her, Sybille Carton. I can call her for both of you.

She may not even be alive now, or too frail. She housed two of our guests last time. They were very happy there. She is a wonderful cook. I hope she's still in business. I'll call her." He disappeared into a back office, and the engineer looked at Darcy with a sympathetic expression. He was calm and friendly as they waited.

"I can pitch a tent if we can't find anything else. It would be quite comfortable," he said, and she smiled.

"You may have to. This all happened so fast. I don't think anyone was prepared for it, even after last time."

"They're smart to do this so quickly. No one wants another mess like last time. This may be the only way to stop it, or so they say." He didn't look worried or frightened and seemed remarkably calm. Darcy wasn't panicked either, but she needed a room somewhere. And clearly, so did he. He was looking her over while appearing not to, and she realized that she was still wearing her wedding ring. She had kept it on because of Zoe. She didn't want to have to explain its absence, although it upset Darcy every time she saw it. She wondered if the confinement might be a good excuse to say that she had put it away, since they had to wash their hands constantly. It was a thin excuse, but Zoe might believe it. The last thing she wanted to do was tell Zoe separately from her twin, or Penny on the phone, and she thought Charlie should do it in person, and she wanted to be with them in the loving cocoon of their home when they heard news that would upset them deeply. Their parents' divorce would be almost as grave as the death of a parent to them.

The manager returned from the back room, and he was smiling. "You're in luck. Madame is eighty-four, she told me. She's still operating, and very selective about who she allows to stay. I explained about both of you, and she was satisfied. And she says she's still cooking. She was quite spry when I last saw her, very active, although it's been several years. Her home is very close to here, in walking distance." It sounded ideal to both of them, as their eyes met, and Darcy nodded.

"I have two heavy suitcases. I'll take a cab," she said.

"I can carry them for you," the engineer offered, and she looked embarrassed.

"Really, they're very heavy."

"I think I can manage." He looked amused. "My name is William Thompson, by the way." He didn't hold out a hand to shake hers because they weren't supposed to. They were back to the old rules from the last pandemic, which they all remembered.

"Mme. Carton will be expecting you whenever you get there. Her rates are somewhat lower than ours. I'm not sure what they are now. She offered a special lowered price in the Covid-19 pandemic. She might be doing that again, and meals are included. She's a very able chef, I hear the meals she prepares are fabulous." Darcy wondered if they'd have to share a bathroom. She hoped not but didn't want to ask. It was the only option available to them in any case, so they'd have to adjust to the arrangement. William Thompson gave the manager a sizable tip, and Darcy did the same, and they both went upstairs to pack their bags so they could move to the new location as soon as possible. People were filling the streets trying to get to places to shelter.

It took Darcy fifteen minutes to get everything back in her suitcases and pack her makeup and toiletries in a tote bag. She was sorry to leave the pretty suite, but the manager's description of the old actress's rooms to rent sounded hopeful. Darcy was back in the lobby, dragging her suitcases behind her out of the elevator minutes later. William Thompson was waiting for her in one of the big chairs in the lobby, with a two-suiter slung over his shoulder, and a small rolling bag next to him. He stood up when he saw her.

"If you pull my rolling bag, I can manage the suitcases," and he didn't look surprised when he saw the size of her bags. They both settled their bills then, left tips for the housekeeping staff, and headed out the door, with Darcy following her new housemate. The address they were going to was a ten-minute walk from the hotel, and William Thompson didn't look in the least troubled by her big suitcases. She always took too many options, and she had wanted to dress up for Charlie, so she had brought more than usual.

"I'm so sorry you have to deal with my bags, Mr. Thompson," she apologized.

"Bill. It's not a problem. It's good exercise." He had powerful arms and seemed very fit. She guessed him to be a few years younger than Charlie, but in much better shape. She wasn't far off the mark, he was forty-nine.

"How long were you in Saudi Arabia?" she asked, to make conversation on the way to their new lodgings. People were rushing around them, hurrying to buy groceries and supplies and get home.

"Two years," Bill said. "I was building supply depots for oil refineries. Several hundred of them." She nodded, and still thought he looked military. They were at the house by then, and Darcy was surprised by how elegant it looked. It was a beautiful, relatively small "hôtel particulier," a townhouse by New York standards, and was about two hundred years old. The front door was painted a shiny black and everything looked in pristine condition and good repair. There was a short hedge around the house and a front garden with red roses. Darcy and Bill walked up to the front door and rang the bell. There was a big brass knocker that seemed more decorative than operational. The door opened quickly, and a small, slightly round older woman with a lovely face, tastefully made-up, with her hair in a snow-white bun, opened the door to them. She was wearing a neat black dress, an immaculate white apron, and a chef's jacket, and she smiled when she saw Darcy and Bill.

"Welcome, please come in," she said with a gracious voice, and stood aside. Darcy thought her face looked faintly familiar, maybe from some old French movies. Her English was impeccable, with a slightly British accent, which was common for French people who had learned English from British teachers.

"I have two guest bedrooms, both on this floor," she explained, "with a parlor between them, for your use. The kitchen, main living room, and dining room are one flight up. You may use the kitchen if you like." She was warm and welcoming, while making the boundaries clear. "And I have two floors above all that, where you won't need to go. Both guest bedrooms are about the same size, one is a little more masculine-looking. The other one is just a few feet larger." Both Bill and Darcy peeked into the rooms she indicated. One had a big four-poster bed, and the other had two big leather chairs and a bookcase. Each room had a desk and plenty of space in elegant antique armoires, and Darcy noticed with relief that each room had its own bathroom. "I added the bathrooms," the woman explained, but they were in keeping with the style of the rest of the house. "No one likes to share a bathroom," she commented with a smile. She seemed like a lovely person, and appeared happy to welcome them.

"Do you have a preference?" Bill Thompson asked Darcy politely. "I've been living in a tent for two years, so I'm easy to please."

"I love the one with the canopied bed," Darcy admitted, and Bill smiled. It looked a fraction larger and had a bigger closet.

"And I like the one with the leather chairs and the bookcase." So, they were off to a good start. Each bedroom had a marble fireplace. The house was so nicely done that it didn't seem like a hotel, but more as though they were houseguests in a beautifully kept home.

"And I don't take credit cards," Mme. Carton added randomly. "I don't know how to work the machine. But a check will do nicely, or cash, whatever you prefer, or a wire. You can pay when you leave. I don't need it before. And meals are included." Darcy couldn't think of a better place to spend the confinement. The chairs in Darcy's room were comfortable enough to read by the fireplace on a chilly night. The room was cozy and inviting.

Bill carried her bags in for her and set them down. There was a single luggage rack, and Mme. Carton said there was a second one in the closet. Bill opened them and set Darcy's bags on them. "I made a little something for your dinner, if you're hungry. I didn't know if you'd have eaten by now, or maybe you didn't have time to, with everything shutting down tonight. I really thought we were finished with this nonsense four years ago, and now here we are again. The hard part is not knowing how long the confinement will last. That was the problem last time too, and people grew impatient. What time would you like to eat?" she asked them.

Neither Bill nor Darcy had other plans, so it didn't matter. Jean-Paul and Zoe were cooking on their own at her apartment.

"We'll say eight o'clock then. I hope you both like hachis parmentier." It was beef layered with mashed potatoes, with truffles shaved into it. It was a rich meal for a winter night, with the delicate flavor of black truffle, and delicious with a green salad. They could both smell irresistible cooking odors coming from the kitchen upstairs.

After Bill set up Darcy's bags in her room, he turned to Mme. Carton and addressed her politely.

"Would you like me to go to the store for you, madame? Do you need groceries or other provisions? Most of the shops will be closed tomorrow except pharmacies and grocery stores. Now's the time to stock up." She thought about it and nodded hesitantly.

"Would you mind?" she asked him.

"Not at all, that's why I asked, and any time while I'm here, please let me know what you need. It's better if you don't go out." Staying home was very strongly urged for people in her age group, and he didn't want to sound rude by implying that she was old. But at eighty-four, she was in the most vulnerable category, who were told not to have visitors at all, even family. She seemed healthy and very active for her years, and moved like a much younger woman than her chronological age. She was grateful for Bill's offer to shop for her.

"I was just working on a list to go myself. I'll get it for you. There's a supermarket three blocks from here. Normally, they'll deliver. I don't know if they will now."

"It's not a problem."

"I'll come with you," Darcy chimed in. "I want to get some things for my daughter. I can take them to her in a cab." There were still plenty of taxis around, although there might not be soon. Zoe never thought of buying food and stocking her kitchen. Darcy was sure she had three bottles of sparkling water and two lemons in the house, and no toilet paper, but plenty of wine to serve her friends, and for her and Jean-Paul to drink when they ordered pizza, when he got home from his shift at the hospital. They were still kids, or she was. Jean-Paul was more grown-up at twenty-six, and had seen many life-and-death situations as a medical student.

Bill and Darcy set out on foot for the store a few minutes later after Mme. Carton gave them her list.

"The house is lovely, isn't it?" Darcy said to Bill on the way. They had both found a discreet note in their rooms with the rate, and it was reasonable and not excessive, especially including gourmet meals.

He smiled as he glanced at her. "After two years in a tent, I'll say it is. I'm in no hurry for my next assignment."

"That sounds pretty rigorous." She was curious about him. None of the elements quite matched up. He still seemed almost military in style to her, as though he was used to wearing a uniform, or had for a long time. He didn't look like an engineer to her, and had a more outgoing personality than most of the engineers she'd met, and had more style. He seemed very observant of his surroundings and the people around him. She had seen him watching people in the lobby of the hotel, and he had taken in every detail of Mme. Carton's elegant house and was very warm and helpful to her. He was different from any man Darcy had met, very American, but with a definitely international aura, and an air of authority about him, as though he was used to command.

"My line of work takes me to areas that have been impacted by either natural disasters or wars. I rebuild them, so conditions are always pretty rugged, particularly when I arrive. By the end, when we have everything up and running, it's quite civil, but it almost always involves living in a tent, or worse. I've spent a lot of time in Iran, Iraq, Afghanistan, and Saudi Arabia. I'm a professional nomad. Speaking of which, you may want to consider going home, while the borders are still open, with your daughter, if it looks like it's going to be a long confinement. Unless you don't mind getting stuck here. Europe was shut down for a long time the last time." As they walked along she noticed that he was handsome, but not in any way flirtatious.

"Were you here then?" She was curious about him.

"I was in China, and moved around a little in Asia. It was very shut down, with strict quarantines." He was an intriguing person, and easy to talk to.

"I have a daughter studying in Hong Kong, and nothing to rush back to in New York." He glanced and saw the wedding ring again, and he wondered where her husband was. He didn't appear to be part of the equation. She never mentioned him. It made him wonder if she was a widow. There was an underlying sadness to her he had noticed in her eyes.

It took them an hour to buy all the groceries and supplies they needed. There were long lines at the store. A lot of things had already run out or been picked over, especially sanitizing products and toilet paper. Mme. Carton wanted quite a lot of fresh food, and Bill wanted easily prepared foods in small portions, obviously planning to eat alone some of the time. Darcy bought as much as she could for

Zoe, and some things she thought Bill and Mme. Carton would enjoy. They had to take a cab back to the house. It was too much to carry.

"You know," he said quietly on the way back, "I don't like being an alarmist, but to shut down the entire country as fast as the French just did, it's probably worse than they're telling people. And every major European country has done the same. I think they all know where we're headed, or where we could be, if they don't move fast. We saw where that led last time." Each country had declared a three- or four-week confinement this time, with the proviso that they would reevaluate circumstances at the end of that period, and no promise to let people out then. "They don't want it to get out of hand, and they're right."

Darcy thought about what he'd said while they unpacked the groceries, wiped them down with the sanitizers they had bought, and threw out the wrappings. Sybille Carton was very grateful to both of them, and very happy with her two guests for the confinement. She had decided not to take anyone in this time when the confinement was announced, but the manager of the Belle Ville had insisted that they both seemed like extremely nice, reasonable people and recommended them highly, and she could see that he was right. Bill had paid for everything on Mme. Carton's list, and Darcy had insisted on chipping in and giving all the extras she had bought for Mme. Carton as a gift.

"I've always liked Americans," Madame had said happily, "they have such big hearts." The statement seemed ironic to Darcy, thinking about Charlie, whose heart was so big he was in love with two women. Maybe his heart was a little too big in his case.

Darcy had set aside the things she'd bought for Zoe, and after they unpacked the groceries for Mme. Carton and the house, she took Zoe her share in a cab. She and Jean-Paul were delighted with what she brought them.

"Thank you, Mom," Zoe said warmly. They'd been watching the evening news and a speech by the French President. Jean-Paul had just received an email from the Faculté de Médecine, assigning him hospital shifts for the next week. There were a lot of them. They wanted to use medical students to do the menial jobs to free up the doctors for the big ones. The memo had also reassured them that they were fully stocked with all the medical supplies they needed—respirators, sanitizers, masks. No country was ever going to risk running short again, not like the last pandemic when countries were begging from each other, desperation set in as ICUs filled up rapidly across the country, and poorly protected medical personnel had gotten sick. Every country had pandemic plans in place now.

Darcy went back to the Carton house just as Zoe was putting a frozen pizza in the oven for dinner. And she got back to Mme. Carton's just in time for the delicious hachis parmentier she'd smelled before. Darcy helped Mme. Carton set a beautiful table when she showed her where the linen placemats were with handmade embroidered linen napkins. She used exquisite china and crystal glasses for dinner. It was better than a three-star restaurant in the Michelin Guide, and when they sat down to eat, the hachis parmentier melted in their mouths. It was a sumptuous meal. Bill had two big servings, and Darcy helped herself to a generous portion. Mme. Carton ate very little, although she was slightly round, so Darcy realized that she must eat well when she was alone, maybe out of boredom, or when she cooked. There were framed photographs from many of her movies, and Darcy was fascinated looking at them. There were a number of them with her director husband, who had been very famous as well. She realized now, looking at the photographs, several of them taken while receiving a César, the French equivalent of an Oscar, that Sybille Carton had been a very big star, but there was nothing arrogant, grand, or pretentious about her. She was a very quiet, unassuming, modest person, and not a diva. And she had a cheerful attitude with her guests.

"She was a *really* big deal," Darcy whispered to Bill, as they headed down to their living room after helping Mme. Carton clean up her kitchen.

"I know," Bill said in an admiring tone. "I've been looking at the photos too. She won two Césars. She worked a lot with her husband."

"I wonder how she wound up running an Airbnb," Darcy said.

"She must need the money," he said coolly, as he sprawled in a big brown antique leather chair Mme. Carton had bought in England. She had bought some beautiful things there, and in France. Darcy and Bill sat down in their shared sitting room. "Her career was a long time ago. I get the feeling she hasn't made a film in twenty years." They looked her up on Google then, and discovered he was right. And she had in fact been a very big star, one of the best actresses in France, and very famous. She had made a few movies in the States and many in other countries in Europe. And she had been gorgeous in her youth.

Bill looked at Darcy then, curious about her too. She'd been planning to read for a while after dinner, but it was more fun talking to him. He had a good sense of humor and had traveled all over the world. He had entertained them at dinner with some very funny stories of places where he'd worked and traveled. "What do you do?" he asked her, a little worried about being intrusive. He was a very private person himself, talking about where he'd worked but with no personal details. She had no idea if he was single or married, or if he had kids.

"I write a blog, and I'm what's now called an 'influencer.' It's a way for companies to engage with their clients. They pay me to promote their products if I believe in them. It sounds a little silly when you say it like that. I write a lot about fashion, but I have other interests too—art, science, decorating, interesting philanthropic causes. I touch on a wide variety of subjects in my blog. I have been doing it for a long time."

"I'm told that bloggers have a great deal of power now through social media." He sounded intrigued.

"That's true," she confirmed. "It depends how you use it. I stay away from politics, but almost everything else interests me. Films, medicine, art. And I only promote what I truly believe in, so people trust me."

"It must be fun. It sounds like you get to wear a lot of hats." He was fascinated by the concept. "I do in my job too, but it can be very dry at times. I'm sure your job never is." She seemed knowledgeable and well informed on a wide variety of subjects, which made her interesting to talk to.

"I'm supposed to be at fashion week, but they canceled it, because of the virus."

"It's a good thing they did. That's the kind of crowded event that can get a whole city sick, or even many cities if it's international." She nodded agreement.

"It's kind of a relief," she admitted, "it's always a madhouse. It goes on for four weeks in four cities. It starts in New York, then London, Milan, and Paris."

There was another thing Bill had been wondering about. Darcy seemed very independent, but her wedding band confused him, she never mentioned her husband. "Is there a Mr. Gray?" he finally asked her directly, and she hesitated and then shook her head.

"Actually, in real life there is a Mr. Gray, but not in my life anymore." She took a quick gulp of air. "We're getting a divorce. We haven't told our daughters yet. We just agreed to separate. In fact, we have been separated for some time. I just didn't know it." She looked sad but resigned as she said it. She was making her peace with it.

"I'm sorry." He looked as though he meant it. There was empathy in his eyes, and she wondered if he was divorced too.

"Are you divorced?" Somehow being confined together allowed one to be more personal. He shook his head.

"No. Widowed. A long time ago, twenty years. We married young, and we'd been married for three years when she got sick. She died of breast cancer at twenty-nine. It went like wildfire. She had a lump, and thought it was nothing. It went to her ovaries, her liver, her brain. I was building bridges in Africa when she got sick. She was a UN nurse. She was kind of a saint, working with displaced kids who'd been orphaned by tribal wars. I never remarried. I became a nomad instead." He smiled at Darcy. He didn't usually talk about it, but she was sympathetic and motherly, and the circumstances led to confessions.

"No kids?" He shook his head again.

"No time. We were busy in Africa. We wanted to do that for five years before we had kids. And kids have always scared me a bit. She would have been better with them than I would. I expect a lot from people, and I run out of patience. My staff thinks I'm hard on them. I was in the Marines before we got married. It kind of stays with you. My father was an admiral." That made total sense to her and was in keeping with his bearing and appearance, and maybe his job.

"That is so weird. I thought there was something military about you when I first saw you."

"I loved it. My wife didn't want to be a Navy wife, so I got out before we got married, and we went to Africa. I almost went back to the Marines after she died, but then I didn't, and ended up doing something else, which worked out fine. I guess you can always tell a Marine." He smiled at her comment. "It can be a great life for the right person. I'm happy being an engineer," he said, and looked content.

He lit a fire in the fireplace in the small sitting room between their bedrooms, and they talked for about an hour, and then he said he had some homework to do, and she went to her bedroom, thinking about him. He seemed solitary, but not lonely. There was a difference. He didn't appear to be pining for a woman's company, and he seemed perfectly at peace with his life, but it was very different taking two-year contracts to rebuild war-torn areas than if he'd had a wife and children and a more normal life in Chicago or Dallas or

Boston, rather than living in a tent in Saudi Arabia for two years. But he didn't seem unhappy about it. To each his own. She thought it was funny that she had sensed something military about him and he was an ex-Marine.

She tried reading a novel before she went to sleep, but she was too distracted, thinking about Zoe in confinement nearby in Paris, Penny in Hong Kong, Charlie with Flavia in Rome. They were under lockdown too, Penny had reported about her father—Darcy had guessed right, he was staying in Rome and not returning to New York. He was obviously with Flavia. Darcy was glad she had decided to stay in Paris, close to Zoe. At least she was near one of her children, if Zoe needed her.

She wondered how Flavia and Charlie were doing, and if he had called his New York lawyers yet to start the divorce. She was waiting to call hers when she got home. She didn't have a divorce lawyer, and would have to call her regular attorney for a referral. As she thought about it, she slowly pulled her wedding band off. She felt as though she were tearing out her heart as she did. She had worn it for twenty years. It had served its purpose, but it was obsolete now. Charlie had made it meaningless. She took it off and laid it in a little dish next to her bed. She was going to put it away in the morning, in a jewel case she traveled with. It was a piece of history now. A relic. A souvenir of the past. She turned off the light then, closed her eyes, and went to sleep. She slept better than she'd expected. She felt safe at Mme. Carton's, with a famous movie star and an ex-Marine.

# Chapter 7

The next morning, Paris was locked down tight, as was all of France and every country in Europe. The United States was shut down too, although they'd had very few cases so far. But that had happened last time as well. It had just started later in the States, and the number of cases was worse than everywhere else because it was such a big country.

Darcy called Zoe, and she and Jean-Paul were doing well, and enjoying the food Darcy had bought. She would have liked to visit them, but it wasn't allowed. No one was to have visitors, to put a really serious, heavy emphasis on the confinement, and have it work to flatten the curve of Co 2-24. In the most recent press conference, the surgeon general had said again that Co 2-24 was less dangerous than Covid-19 but could still be fatal. They were estimating that, at worst, less than one percent of the world population would die of it, fewer than had died of the Spanish flu in 1918, or significantly less if a vaccine was found quickly. It was as highly contagious as

Covid-19, but there were medications which were believed to miti-
gate it. None were in use so far, as the protocols were not fully per-
fected, but there was hope on the horizon. Researchers were working
frantically to find a vaccine, but the news anchor said it would be
months or even a few years away. Until then, everyone was at risk.
Many people were able to stave off or diminish the effects of the new
virus with the medications they were trying, but the news did not
deny that many people would die worldwide before it was over. And
much of the information was contradictory. Flavia couldn't watch the
news anymore. It was too stressful for her. Spokespersons for the
government said that they believed the virus would come and go in
a month if everyone stayed in confinement. They wanted to stop it
fast and thought they could, if strict lockdown was observed. The
population of every city had to comply and follow the rules. America
was a big country, and compliance was hard to enforce in a country
that size. There was a terrible déjà vu to it after Covid-19.

Every night, Darcy and Bill had dinner with Sybille Carton while she
told them stories of the past, of her movie career and visits to Hollywood. She was a fountain of wisdom and amusing stories that never
dried up. She enjoyed their company, and afterward, when she went
to bed, it was becoming a ritual that Bill and Darcy played cards,
dominoes, and Scrabble in the little parlor they shared on the main
floor, and chatted while they did. They learned a great deal about
each other, their jobs, their families, and Darcy's children, and finally
one day she told Bill about Charlie's betrayal, his life with Flavia, and
soon their baby.

"Wow, I'm not sure if doing that takes guts, or is a sign of immense cowardice. Being dedicated to one woman is a huge commitment I've never felt equal to again. I can't even imagine what two must be like, while lying and hiding one from the other. He must have been in denial and thought he'd never get caught. And you haven't told your children?" He was surprised by that, it seemed like loyalty above and beyond the call of duty to her ex-husband, who didn't deserve it, in Bill's opinion. He had no respect for a man who had done what Charlie did and felt sorry for Darcy. She sounded amazingly decent about it. There was a kindness and compassion about her which he admired, and grace under fire, like during their confinement.

"I wanted to wait until both girls were back, so I could be there to support them when he tells them together. That won't be till June, and they'll need our full support. They're all spread out now in different cities. It wouldn't be fair to tell them now, on the phone. I want them home with me when we tell them. Even at nineteen, the divorce will be a big deal to them. They don't expect it. Neither did I. It seems wrong to tell them while we're in confinement, and the girls are apart, and me too."

"And they won't figure it out?" He was surprised.

"They might. He should really be the one to tell them. I don't know if he will or not. He's hard to predict, to say the least." And waiting didn't matter. He had been cheating for two years. Telling the girls in June wouldn't make much difference.

Several days into their confinement, Bill noticed that she was no longer wearing her wedding ring. He could understand why now and didn't comment, but she seemed less sad and devastated than when he had first seen her. She was working on her blog during the confinement, keeping up with posting for her clients on social media, and talking about the different ways people were handling being confined again. She spoke to several psychiatrists and incorporated their suggestions. All of the French designers whose shows had been canceled showed their collections online, in sketches or on hangers, and orders were being taken. Once again, economies around the world were being impacted, the stock markets plummeted, and Darcy interviewed a series of America's most respected investment advisers and analysts over the phone.

Bill was keeping busy too. He had a number of Zoom and video meetings. His bedroom door was closed for most of the day, and she knew he was working. They met for dinner at night in Mme. Carton's big friendly kitchen for another of her delicious meals. Darcy had put several of Mme. Carton's recipes on her blog, and she started taking cooking lessons from her. Darcy was fascinated by the magic of Madame's cooking—she was a really talented chef, and her soufflés, both sweet and savory, were sublime. Darcy mastered them in two lessons with Madame's simple, clear instructions.

Somehow, the days passed, and people in every country found ways to keep busy. Bill became fascinated by her blog and compared her to a one-man newspaper, incorporating a multitude of subjects and bringing a wealth of information to her followers. People loved it, and he said he was becoming addicted to it. It entertained as well as informed, and had Darcy's particular, very distinctive spin on it, though she tried to be objective, presenting experts and opinions from all sides of an argument to give her readers perspective and an opportunity to form their own opinions. He particularly liked that about it. She didn't impose her point of view, she shared many, so her followers could choose their own from the data available.

Bill didn't talk to her about his own work, but he was always friendly and personable when they met up at night at Sybille Carton's table for a delicious meal, and afterward when he and Darcy talked in their little sitting room after Sybille went to bed. She was something of a grande dame, but a very kind one, and both were aware that she was at great risk from the virus, since she was among the population considered the most vulnerable and the least likely to survive the virus, although she was in excellent health. She was brave and philosophical and didn't seem afraid.

Within days, the virus had taken hold and the number of people sick with it in ICUs in hospitals around the world, and the death toll, were shocking. Co 2-24 had taken off even faster than Covid-19 four years earlier. Fewer people were dying of it, but within two weeks, people were critically ill in every country around the globe. Each country was better prepared for it than they had been before, but the impact it had was horrifying. People were panicked and terrified, and it was harder every day to remain hopeful that the world would survive it, and there was an underlying anxiety to each moment of the day.

Darcy was talking to Zoe about it one day on the phone in the second week of their confinement, while Jean-Paul was at the Pitié-Salpétrière Hospital for one of his assigned shifts. The death toll had been mounting exponentially for several days, and Zoe worried about him doing his shifts, even though there were enough gloves and masks this time, and even respirators.

"What's Dad saying about all this now?" Zoe asked her. "I haven't spoken to him in a few days. How is it in Italy?"

"About the same as it is here," Darcy said quietly, from statistics she'd seen. She hadn't spoken to Charlie, which she didn't say to Zoe. Their daughters still suspected nothing. Their separation seemed like too much to add with the world falling apart around them—again. Zoe and Penny were young to have faced two pandemics in their brief lifetimes.

"He must have finished work there by now. Why doesn't Dad come here? He could stay with you, Mom," Zoe suggested. "That would be nicer for you." Darcy made no comment, and stayed silent a fraction of a second longer than she should have. Zoe picked up on it immediately. "Wouldn't that be better for you?"

"The room's a little small, and the woman who owns the house is very old, she may not want to be exposed to another person, coming from another country. And I'm not sure he'd like it here. I'm pretty sure the border is closed now between France and Italy. He's probably better off there, with people he knows." The Hassler had closed, and she was sure that he was staying with Flavia. They hadn't spoken since she had left Rome, and she didn't want to talk to him. He hadn't called her either. He had sent a text, asking if she was okay. From now on, she preferred to deal with him through their attorneys, once she had one. There was nothing more to say on a personal level. Zoe had picked up on the undertone in her mother's voice. Penny wouldn't have. Zoe was more finely tuned at picking up nuances, and more suspicious. Penny was more inclined to believe that everything was okay, as their mother claimed.

"Mom? Is something wrong with you and Dad?" Zoe asked her. Darcy didn't want to outright lie to her, they were delicate waters to navigate.

She didn't answer the question directly. "He's been really busy, and with the lockdown and everything, I'm sure it's been crazy."

"That's not what I asked you. Are you and Dad having a problem? Did you have a fight when you went to Rome?" The question was as direct as Zoe could make it. Her alarm bells had sounded as soon as her mother arrived in Paris.

"Yeah, we've run into some problems. This really isn't the right time to deal with it. We're letting it sit till we all get home," which was relatively true.

"Are you and Dad breaking up?" Zoe sounded horrified, and Darcy didn't want to have to tell her.

"Let's let that be for now. We can't deal with serious issues with all of us spread all over the world."

"*Is* there a serious issue?" Zoe asked pointedly.

"There might be. You really need to talk to your father about it." After they hung up, Zoe called her father, and it kept going to voice-mail, which meant that he was probably on a business call, which could last for hours, so she called Penny in Hong Kong.

"911," Zoe told Penny when she answered. "Mom doesn't want to talk about it, but she's hiding something, there's some kind of serious issue with Dad."

"Zoe, the whole world is having serious issues. They're probably just stressed out and worried. They're not even together right now in the same city."

"No, and they don't want to be. Penny, stop being such a Goody Two-shoes and listen to me. I think they might be splitting up."

"I don't believe it. You're overreacting. You always do that."

"I'm not. I'll talk to Dad about it and let you know."

Charlie called Zoe back an hour later when he got off a Zoom call at Flavia's house in Rome. He had been on the phone all day, making business calls. Flavia didn't even see him till dinnertime. Zoe asked him the same question she'd asked their mother.

"Are you and Mom splitting up?" She got right to the point and there was silence at his end while her eyes grew wide and her stomach tightened.

"We've run into some problems. I don't want to discuss it now, on the phone. We'll talk about it when we all get home. Right now, just stay inside, be safe, and take care of yourself."

"Dad, what happened?" Tears sprang to her eyes, and he felt terrible at the fear he could hear in her voice.

"Let's not go there now. I love you, Zoe."

"I love you too," she told her father. "Is there anything I can do to help?"

"Just stay safe," he repeated. "Your mother and I love both of you, that's all that matters."

"I love you too, Dad," she said, and a minute later they hung up and she called Penny again, crying this time. Penny tried to comfort her and reassure her, to no avail.

"They're not going to split up now after all this time. This is stressful. Dad's worried about the stores again. They're probably just snapping at each other."

"Dad says they're having problems and we'll talk about it when we all get home, which is pretty much what Mom said too."

"I'm sure they'll be fine by then. Just relax and have some fun with Jean-Paul."

"He's exhausted when he comes back from his shifts, and he says this new virus is much worse than they're telling us, and a lot of young people are dying too. More than old ones this time. It's damaging people's hearts."

"Just take it easy and slow down. You're stressed out. And stop worrying about Mom and Dad." Penny always had a soothing effect on her. It was Zoe who was the most high-strung. "Go do your relaxation exercises. Promise?"

"Yeah, okay," Zoe said grudgingly. "You really think they'll be okay?"

"I promise they'll be fine." They hung up a few minutes later, and Zoe lay down on the couch to do her breathing exercises while she waited for Jean-Paul to come home, and when he got back, she was asleep. He had seen two children die that day. He didn't wake Zoe. He went to bed and cried himself to sleep.

Darcy continued to take cooking lessons with Mme. Carton, and wrote about it on her blog. The numbers of sick and dead continued to mount in France and around the world, and the tension was unbearable. She and Bill talked about the numbers every day before he started work. He was in meetings on the phone all day, and always kept his bedroom door closed when he was. But the numbers were frightening. The governments had said that this virus wouldn't be as lethal as Covid-19, but it nearly was, and it had just started. They said it would be over faster, which remained to be seen. The cooking lessons calmed Darcy, and she loved spending time with the beautiful old actress who had seen a lot in her lifetime, and was very wise.

She was teaching Darcy how to make all her favorite French dishes. She was showing her how to make *confit de canard.* Darcy watched her carefully, wrote the directions down diligently, and shared them afterward on her blog. And on some nights, she tried them out on Bill and Mme. Carton. So far, it was the most enjoyable part of the confinement, and Bill was enjoying it too. He was complaining that he was gaining weight. He did push-ups morning and night to try to counteract the delicious food.

"You know, he reminds me of someone," Sybille Carton said, as she demonstrated to Darcy how to prepare the duck.

"Who does he remind you of?" Darcy asked her. She had a rich treasure trove of funny incidents, famous friends, and remarkable people she had met. In sixty-five years as an actress, she had seen many things. Darcy wasn't sure who Sybille was talking about, but she waited for the story.

"I can't remember his name. We were in a movie together in L.A., my first American movie. I was about twenty-five. It was during the Cold War. I had dinner with him a few times—he was very good-looking, and quite mysterious. I always had the feeling that he had something of a double life. He stood me up a few times, and I eventually got bored with him. I heard later that he gave up acting, and the director we worked with told me he was a spy and worked for the CIA. Howard Green!" she said, as the name popped back into her memory, and she beamed at Darcy. "Howard Green. Bill reminds me of him. He even looks like him. Maybe Bill is a spy, or works for the CIA." Darcy almost laughed, but forced herself not to.

"I don't think he's a spy. He's an engineer."

"Spies always have other careers as a cover. He's traveled too much in interesting, dangerous places. Who do you know who spends two years in Saudi Arabia, living in a tent, and supposedly building little huts or digging a ditch or some other unlikely story. He's a spy," Madame said firmly, and they both laughed.

"Should we ask him?" Darcy teased her.

"He wouldn't tell us the truth," Mme. Carton said sensibly. That much Darcy agreed with, but there was no way that Bill was a spy or an agent of the CIA. He was a normal reasonable person, an engineer in a not-very-exciting job, who had spent his life working in the Middle East after his wife died, and in Africa in his youth. He was a nomad, as he said, not a spy. It all made sense to her. But Mme. Carton's theory was more fun. And Darcy teased her about it as they made exquisite duck. Darcy had made note of every step and wanted to do it again. Bill was their guinea pig for Darcy's cooking lessons, and definitely not CIA. But the theory was fun. She almost wanted to tell him so he'd have a good laugh. But she didn't know if he'd think it was funny or be annoyed, so she didn't tell him. Mme. Carton loved the idea and repeated it at the end of the lesson. "Well, our favorite spy will have a beautiful duck dinner tonight!" she said, with a twinkle in her eye, and Darcy laughed again, thinking about it, on the way back to her room, to write down the recipe in her computer for her blog. Bill's door was closed when she walked past his room, and she smiled thinking about how amusing it was that Mme. Carton thought he was a spy.

In Italy, Charlie was living with Flavia for the confinement, and Roberto had moved in with his parents again. He preferred staying in their big house to being alone in his apartment. His parents' maids and houseman were confined with them, so there were people to take care of him.

Bianca, Paolo, and their three little boys had moved into the Tedesco villa too. Stella and her family had preferred to stay in their own home. And they all got together for dinner every night, which violated the rules of the confinement, but they knew many families who did that in Rome. Italian families stayed together in hard times, although the practice had fanned the flames of the contagion during the Covid pandemic and had caused several members of the same family to die as a result. If one member of the family caught it, they all did, because they were so exposed to each other during the asymptomatic incubation period. Charlie had complained to Flavia about it, when he realized that they expected him and Flavia to join them for dinner every night.

"That's dangerous, Flavia. It defeats the purpose of the confinement. We're supposed to be staying away from other people to save lives."

"We're Italian," she said and kissed him. "Italian families stay together all the time, especially if something bad is happening. We stick together."

"But you can make each other sick, if one of you has been exposed to the virus and you don't know that. And I don't want them to make you sick, especially while you're pregnant. I don't want to have dinner with them, and I don't want them coming to your house." She looked shocked.

"I can't tell them that, Charlie. They'd be insulted. And my father will be very upset if we don't come to dinner."

"He'll be more than upset if someone in the family dies because you're not respecting the confinement. Flavia, Italy had some of the worst numbers in the world last time after the U.S. and China, and it'll happen again if they keep having family gatherings. I won't let you go." She looked angry for a minute, stormed off to their bedroom, shouted at him that he didn't understand anything, and slammed the door. She came back an hour later, looking calmer. She had thought about it and wondered if he was right. Her brother and sister-in-law had died in the last one, and the family had been heartbroken. She didn't want it happening again. And it might have been more than coincidence. The aunt and uncle who had died had been dining with the aunt's family every day, along with her ancient mother, seven brothers, and their wives and children. Several of them had died early in the last pandemic.

"Maybe you're right," she conceded, and they canceled going to dinner that night. It made her think of something else. Francesca, her mother, wanted to bring her own mother down from Florence to stay at the house with them. Francesca's older sister, Flavia's aunt, was too terrified to leave her house and go out, and Flavia's grandmother was alone with her ancient servants, and Francesca thought it would be better to bring her to Rome, so she could enjoy the family and the children and be distracted. Flavia asked Charlie what he thought about it, and he was emphatic.

"You should leave your grandmother where she is, and the fewer people she sees, the better. If one of your family gets the new virus, it could kill her. You have to follow the rules. I know this is Italy, and family is everything, so let's try to keep everyone safe, especially you."

Flavia called her mother and explained it all to her, and Francesca said she would explain it to Umberto, but she thought he'd be upset if Flavia and Charlie stayed away. He didn't believe that contagion in the family had killed Pietro. He was sure he had caught it from some random person in the street, or when they shopped for food.

Umberto called Flavia the next morning and insisted that he wanted them to come to dinner that night. It was Massimo's birthday, and he'd be insulted if they didn't come. Flavia explained Charlie's whole theory to him herself and said that she agreed, and it seemed best that they not come. In the end, he lost his temper and hung up on her in a fury. But they didn't go that night, and from then on they stayed home and saw no one. Charlie was relieved, and Flavia was in the family's black books for listening to him. But she somehow managed to convince her mother to leave Nonna Graziella in Florence, which Charlie said might save her life. As for all the others in the family, Charlie insisted that they were risking each others' lives and their own every day at lunch and dinner, crowded around the big dining table, laughing and talking, and passing platters from one end of the table to the other. Umberto didn't believe that they could infect each other.

"Families don't make each other sick," he insisted, and he was angry at Charlie for keeping Flavia from them, but from everything he'd read, Charlie was sure he was doing the right thing. He had urged Zoe to be just as careful in Paris, and Penny in Hong Kong. He hoped that Darcy was safe and he was worried about her, but she didn't answer his texts. Zoe said she was safe in a luxurious Airbnb confined with only two other people, and not going out. Charlie was relieved to hear it, and was sorry he couldn't reason with Umberto. As the head of the family, his word was law, and they followed him blindly as the numbers rose like rockets in Italy, in Europe, in the U.S., and all over the world. Charlie and Flavia closed their doors to the world and the family and stayed home. He was glad he was there to protect her, and their unborn son.

# Chapter 8

When Mariette Nattier heard that they were about to be confined immediately in France, she had to send her domestic employees home and shut down her factories. She was about to spend several weeks or a month confined with her husband. It sounded like a fate worse than death to her. With no children, she could never explain to herself why she and Philippe had stayed married, other than laziness or not wanting to untangle and disengage their financial affairs. Both she and Philippe had established successful businesses of their own. They had led separate lives and had separate bedrooms for thirty years, and each had had several serious romantic liaisons, but none of them serious enough to want to get divorced. Mariette was sixty-two, a once sexy, slightly overweight artificial blonde, and Philippe sixty-nine, mostly bald with a sizable paunch. Their ages put them both in the category of those most vulnerable to the virus, and least likely to survive if they caught it, according to initial estimations, similar to last time in Philippe's case, not hers.

She couldn't remember the last time she had a lengthy conversation with her husband, spent a weekend with him, or shared a meal, let alone been locked in a house alone together for an indeterminate amount of time. She felt nearly suicidal at the thought, and Philippe wasn't pleased at the prospect either. And worse yet, they both had to shut their factories down, since neither of their businesses qualified as essential, and they couldn't risk their factory workers' lives. They both intended to try to have meetings and work remotely.

She owned the most successful perfume factories in France, and she was consulted by perfume manufacturers all over the world. Philippe had been an inventor who had had no success with any of his projects until he turned fifty. And then twenty years ago he had had what became legendary success, at first with a remarkable hair dryer, then with heaters and fans, and household appliances that were much more efficient than any ever made before. They sold for ten times the usual price and were snapped up as though they were giving them away. Nattier products were considered a stroke of genius, and Philippe had made millions. But his hair dryers and vacuum cleaners weren't considered "essential" products either, so his factories were also now closed. Other than Zoom meetings they each organized several times a day, he and his wife were stuck looking at each other and having to be far more civil than they had been to each other in several decades.

Their successful businesses had kept them legally married so as not to lose half of their fortunes in a divorce, but hadn't improved the quality of their relationship, and Mariette was well aware that Philippe had a new Russian mistress who was twenty-three years old and costing him a fortune. He hadn't given Mariette a gift, let alone an Hermès crocodile bag, in thirty years. He had just given Olga, his Russian girlfriend, four, with diamond-encrusted hardware. Mariette had seen the girl on her Instagram wearing one, and holding the other three, once Mariette knew her name and looked her up on Instagram. None of this delighted either of them when they learned they had to close the doors to their Paris home for unlimited confinement. They lived in a beautiful eighteenth-century house on the Rue de Grenelle in the 7th arrondissement.

Philippe had taken over the dining room as his office, and Mariette the library as hers. They met in the kitchen as they each prepared a meal for themselves, greeted each other politely, and took the plates they had prepared with them to eat alone elsewhere in the house, which they both felt was better than trying to make small talk with someone who had become a virtual stranger, and whom they hadn't liked for years. Neither of them was a good cook. Philippe was living on sausages and red wine, and Mariette on scrambled eggs and pastry.

They'd been in confinement for a week when Philippe wandered into the library where Mariette was working, looking somewhat forlorn. Olga had just told him that she was going back to Russia since she had nowhere to continue to live in Paris, and she couldn't stay with him. He had put her up at the Four Seasons for the past month, and the hotel was now closed. She had run out of friends to camp with. Everyone was afraid of contagion, and Olga had been staying with different friends every night, so she was an obvious risk no one wanted to have in their home. And Russia had opened their borders to their citizens who wanted to come. She'd have to quarantine for several weeks once she got home.

"I assume your factories are all closed now?" Philippe said to Mariette, sitting down across from her in the library. He was wearing pajamas and a bathrobe, which he seemed to wear every day now, except when he had Zoom meetings. She hadn't seen him in his nightclothes in years. She was wearing jogging pants with an old sweater, and her blond, chicly cut hair was beginning to show black roots peppered with gray.

She nodded. "Yours must be closed now too."

"We survived the pandemic four years ago, we recouped our losses, and have multiplied our bottom line incredibly, and now we get hit again. I hope it doesn't put me out of business." She smiled. He had always been a worrier, even after he became rich.

"You don't need to worry. People are always going to need hair dryers and vacuum cleaners. In contrast, no one 'needs' perfume. I may be the one to go out of business." Mariette's family had been the most important perfume makers in France since the court of Louis XV, and she had inherited the business when her father died. She had a brother who died before him, so she was the only heir.

"You're an institution. You'll bounce back very quickly," he reassured her. Business was what they both cared about most in lieu of children, since they had none.

It was the friendliest exchange they'd had in years. She offered to make him dinner that night, and he was touched. They sat down to an omelet together in the kitchen, and he told her how pretty she looked, and complimented her on her figure. She had a trainer five days a week, and she was meeting him on Skype during the confinement. After the omelet, they drank Château d'Yquem together and accidentally almost wound up in the same bedroom. Confinement made for strange bedfellows and partnerships. She kissed him on the cheek and then went to her own bedroom, as always.

The numbers reported on the news of those contaminated were staggering. Things were turning ugly fast in every country in Europe, and it was starting to explode in Asia and the United States. It still wasn't as bad as the coronavirus, but the potential was there, if it got out of hand. There were helpful medications this time to curb the effects, but also the possibility that worldwide, they could run out. Production couldn't keep up with the demand.

Charlie and Flavia cooked dinner together. He was trying to master the art of pasta carbonara. They sat down to eat, and he was pleased to see that she was eating well. She had been working remotely all day with Zoom meetings and so had he, and they tried to relax together in the evening.

They had just finished dinner when Roberto called Flavia to tell her their father wasn't feeling well, and their mother thought he should go to the hospital. He was refusing to go.

"Is that a good idea?" Flavia said, instantly worried, as Charlie listened to her side of the conversation, and understood enough Italian now to get the gist of it. He still wasn't fluent, and Flavia's family spoke enough English that he didn't need to be. And he took a translator with him to meetings. Flavia was talking about her "Babbo," her daddy. They all called him that, even Roberto. "There are so many sick people at the hospital. He might catch something worse than he has. Did you call his doctor?" she asked Roberto. And Charlie understood that too.

"He's in Milan for two days, and Babbo doesn't want to see his replacement," Roberto explained.

"He has to. We need to know if he has the virus, and if he should be in the hospital if he does."

"He says it's not the virus." Their father was stubborn even at the best of times.

"He's not a doctor Berto. Just call the doctor and ask him to come to the house. Someone should see him. He's seventy-eight years old."

"I know how old he is," Roberto said, annoyed. "He wants to see you." When he said it, Flavia glanced at Charlie, as though he could hear it, but he didn't. "He's upset that the two of you haven't been coming to dinner."

"Charlie's right, we shouldn't be together. This virus is supposedly even more contagious than the last one. If one of us gets it, we all will. And I'm pregnant."

"So is Bianca, and she's not complaining. She and Massimo and the kids are all living right in the house."

"And you're all exposing each other. The whole point of confinement is to stay away from other people. And you all sit on top of each other at the table, and hug and kiss each other." Charlie had finally convinced her, and after reading more, she fully understood how dangerous it was, and now her father was sick.

"We're not 'other people,' we're a family," Roberto said, irritated.

"And what you're doing is dangerous. Tell Babbo I can't come, that my doctor told me not to." She hadn't asked him, but she was sure he would. "And families can make each other sick." She was certain now that that was how Pietro and his wife had gotten Covid-19. It was a miracle the others hadn't gotten it too.

"Will you call him and talk to him? He needs to see a doctor." She hung up quickly and filled Charlie in.

"My father's sick and he doesn't want to see a doctor or go to the hospital."

"How sick?" Charlie asked, worried. It had only been a week since they'd last had dinner with Umberto, and if he had the virus, they had all been exposed to him. With their sloppy confinement practices, they were a tragedy waiting to happen.

"Sick enough for my mother and Roberto to think he should be in the hospital, or at least see a doctor." She called her father then, and he told her how sad he was that she hadn't come to dinner to see them all, and they all missed her. Like Roberto, he reminded her that her sister was pregnant too, and hadn't isolated herself from them.

"That's what we're all supposed to do, Babbo. You too. You're vulnerable. Mama wants you to see a doctor," she said gently. "Don't worry her. Why don't you let her call a doctor?" He grumbled about it, grudgingly agreed, and reminded her to come to dinner soon. She called Roberto back and told him he had agreed to see a doctor. "Call me after he sees the doctor," she told Roberto. He texted her an hour later that the doctor hadn't come, but said to keep an eye on him, and call if he got any worse. Most doctors were trying not to make house calls and diagnosed by phone.

Flavia was worried when they went to bed that night, but hoped her father wouldn't get any sicker, and might only have caught a mild case of the virus. She slept lightly that night, with one ear listening for the phone.

Roberto called her at four A.M. She and Charlie both gave a start when it rang, and she answered it immediately.

"I just took him to the hospital," Roberto told her. "He was having trouble seeing, he couldn't breathe, he has a fever, and he started having chest pains." It didn't sound good, and Roberto was crying. "They wouldn't let me stay with him. No relatives can stay with the patients, not even spouses."

"Is Mama with you?" She hoped not. Their mother was vulnerable too, although she was younger than Umberto, but she was still over the age they worried about.

"No, I didn't let her come," Roberto reassured her. "They said they'd call me if there was any change." After they hung up, Flavia thought as she had before about all the doctors and nurses who were risking their lives to take care of all the virus patients, with inadequate means and material to protect themselves. Their situation was better than it had been four years ago after many fund drives for supplies for them, but they still didn't have enough. "I'll call you if I hear anything. He's in the ICU. They won't let any of us be with him." She had heard about that before from others. No patient could have visitors, even if they were dying.

Flavia couldn't sleep for the rest of the night, worrying about her father, and Roberto had been exposed now too, helping to get him to the hospital. And she thought of all the exposure the whole family had had before. None of them had taken the rules of the confinement seriously within the family. Charlie lay next to her with his arm around her. They both fell asleep until the phone rang again at nine A.M.

It was Roberto calling to report on their father. Someone in the ICU had finally answered the phone. They said that his father had

had a peaceful night, and there was no change in his condition. He had been tested and had the virus, which had been obvious from his symptoms.

"Try to get some rest," she told Roberto. "And make sure the girls stay with Mama. She's going to be very upset that she can't see him and he can't have visitors."

"She already is," Roberto said, sounding exhausted. He'd been up all night. And Flavia kept thinking that all of them had been exposed and were at high risk of catching the virus. She and Charlie had been exposed too, the last time they had dinner with them. It made her grateful again that her mother hadn't brought Nonna Graziella from Florence to stay with them. At her age, it could have been a death sentence, although not every elderly person caught the virus, and even when they did, not all of them died. She just hoped her father would survive it. She got up to start her day. She had a meeting in an hour, and a lot on her mind, worrying about her father in the hospital. It reminded her far too much of four years before, when her older brother got sick. All she could do now was pray her father would be spared, and that none of the others had caught it from him, and she and Charlie hadn't either, but neither of them were sick after a week. The others had been exposed every day since.

When Darcy got up in Paris, she called Zoe, who was upset. Jean-Paul had been assigned a three-day shift in the hospital, to assist wherever he could. The hospital was overcrowded and understaffed, every bed was full, and nurses and doctors were getting sick. Zoe was terrified he'd catch the virus, and apparently they were starting to run short of protective gear. The new virus had a shorter incubation period than Covid-19 so most people got sick within less than a week of exposure. And only a few rare cases took a week longer to declare themselves, as long as fourteen days, like Covid-19.

Darcy tried to reassure Zoe that Jean-Paul was young and healthy and knew how to protect himself, and he'd be fine. She hoped that that was true.

She had a cup of coffee in the kitchen, and went out for a run to clear her head and get some air. You could only walk or jog within a short distance of your home, and couldn't stay out longer than half an hour. She wanted some exercise before she started work on her blog. She was surprised to see Bill Thompson running, after she'd been out for ten minutes. She came up alongside him and kept the proper distance. She didn't know if he'd want company or not and didn't want to be a nuisance.

"You're out early," he commented, as they ran, close enough to talk.

"I've got a lot of work to do today." She had gotten some interesting summaries of medical information for her blog and wanted to distill it for her readers. It was about symptoms, possible new remedies, and confinement protocols. "I have a lot of meetings today."

"Me too," he said quietly. "Want to run the last few blocks together?" he invited her, and she nodded with a smile. They were fairly evenly matched in their pace, it was comfortable running next to him, and they got back to the Carton house at the same time. She had long legs and was a smooth, fast runner.

They had a cup of coffee together in the kitchen, and then they both went downstairs to their rooms to work. He had more high-tech computer equipment than she did, and Mme. Carton had equipped the house well to support Wi-Fi and whatever connections her guests needed. They'd had no technical problems since they'd been there. He always closed his door when he was working, and Darcy smiled, thinking of Mme. Carton's suspicions that he was a spy, which Darcy considered extremely unlikely. Then she got to work reading the medical reports for her blog. Fashion had been put in the background for now, and she was trying to supply her followers with all the information they wanted about the Co 2-24 virus.

It seemed to move faster than Covid-19, with a shorter incubation, and in severe cases, worsened more rapidly. A higher percentage of people were surviving. It was no respecter of age, and young and old were dying. Everyone hoped that it would end sooner than the coronavirus, which had become rare and far less lethal now, but it still hadn't disappeared completely. But it had become far less dangerous over time, with the entire population of every country in confinement. This time, everyone hoped it would be of short duration and dissipate quickly.

As she started working, Darcy thought of Jean-Paul on his shift at the hospital, and hoped he would be okay. Life was so uncertain now. No one knew if they would be one of the lucky ones and survive, or if their loved ones would. It added a constant, subterranean layer of stress and anxiety to every day, and made it extremely difficult to concentrate on work or anything else. But she felt a responsibility to keep her followers as well informed as she could, so she pressed on. It kept her busy and her mind off herself and her daughters.

# Chapter 9

Philippe Nattier woke Mariette early in the morning. She looked tired and had a cough when he gently shook her awake.

"Are you sick?" He looked worried.

"No, I'm fine."

"I had an idea. What if you opened your factories to provide all the disinfectant and hand sanitizer that's needed. You have enormous production capacity if you open all of them, or even one." She lay in bed, thinking about it. It was certainly feasible, and would help people if she did. And Philippe was considering opening his factories to produce the respirators and ventilators they were starting to run short of again, as they had last time, and defibrillators. The new virus attacked its victims' hearts primarily, and occasionally lungs too.

They both spent the morning on the phone, organizing it, and by that night, their factories would be open in the next two days providing needed supplies to care for the people who were sick, save lives, and prevent the transmission of the illness.

Mariette was coughing more by the end of the day, and had a fever when she took her temperature, and Philippe looked panicked. "Oh my God, you have it. Should I take you to the hospital?"

"No, I'll be okay," she wheezed, and coughed. She didn't want to frighten him, but she felt awful. She called her doctor and he said to stay home for now.

Philippe sat next to her bed and held her hand that night, and she smiled as she drifted off to sleep. It was so comforting to have him there. It was nice to be on friendly terms with him again. She had forgotten what a decent guy he could be at times. And she liked the idea that their factories were serving a useful purpose now.

The news they had been dreading came in Italy that night. Umberto, Flavia's father, had been in the hospital for three days, when all his vital organs suddenly failed, his heart, kidneys, and lungs. He died alone, without any member of his family present, according to the rules, which went against everything their family stood for. Funerals were forbidden until after the epidemic was over. They were told that his ashes would be returned to them in an urn, when the mortuaries were less overwhelmed.

The family got together to mourn, unable to believe what had happened. Flavia's mother, Francesca, was inconsolable, as were her four children. Stella called to tell them that her ten-year-old son had a mild case and may have infected all of them in the past two weeks, in addition to Umberto. It was strongly discouraged to have close contact with children, because they were thought to be carriers, but the Tedescos had allowed them to play in their midst and come to family meals anyway.

Flavia was the only family member who hadn't been there at meals because she had stayed home at Charlie's insistence, and they were both relieved that she'd listened to him. She was panicked for her mother, who had been babysitting for the grandchildren since the confinement began, even though people her age weren't supposed to. And she had spent every moment, night and day, with Umberto. Now that he had died, Francesca said she hoped she would die too. It was a grim night for the Tedescos. None of them could imagine the family without Umberto. They had lost another cousin of her father's two days before, who was ninety. They had lost a brother and several cousins to Covid-19, and Francesca's oldest son and daughter-in-law, and now a beloved husband, father, and grandfather to the new virus. It had been dangerous for all of them to spend so much time together during the confinement, and if Charlie hadn't objected, Flavia would have continued having dinner with them every night. Being a close-knit family was at the root of their culture, and they refused to understand how dangerous it was for them to be together. Social distancing was incomprehensible to them.

Charlie was terrified for Flavia and their unborn baby, and that one of the family might have infected her. Even Bianca was finally starting to worry about it. Her husband began to show symptoms the day after Umberto died, and she made him quarantine in a separate room and not join them for meals. Stella kept her youngest son at her home, because he had been confirmed to have the virus, but he had been at every family meal until then.

The kind of close family contact they had maintained had wiped out entire families during the pandemic of Covid-19. It wasn't as severe this time, but just among the Tedescos there were three cases now, Umberto, Stella's son, and Bianca's husband. Charlie prayed that Flavia wouldn't be the next one to show symptoms, but she had been more careful than any of them, at his insistence.

With the exception of Stella, who was nursing her son, and Flavia, who was staying home with Charlie, they all got together at the house to say prayers for Umberto. They sat a little less close together than usual, and it was a somber afternoon as Roberto led them in prayer. They lit candles for him, and Bianca sang "Ave Maria," which Umberto had loved, in her strong pure voice. No formal funerals were allowed during the confinement, and no burials. All the churches were closed. The mortuaries were cremating the bodies to return the ashes to families after the epidemic was over.

Flavia sat quietly at home, praying for her father. She couldn't imagine her life without him. None of them could. Roberto would have to step into his shoes as the head of the company, with Stella to help him. Umberto's were big shoes to fill, and it would take all of them to do it.

Francesca was inconsolable. She and Umberto had been married for forty-seven years. Without him, their family would never be the same again. And he was much too young to die at seventy-eight.

Three days after she'd last spoken to her, Darcy got a tearful call from Zoe. Jean-Paul had done his three-day shift at the hospital, but it had ended two days before, and he hadn't come home yet. He always called if he was delayed. He was prompt and reliable. She hadn't heard from him and she was terrified that something had happened to him or that he was sick. Darcy reassured her that they had probably made him stay for extra days, if everything the news said was true. The numbers of sick and the death counts were rising dramatically daily. The situation in the hospitals was dire, with too few ICU beds, and exhausted doctors and health workers, unable to protect themselves adequately and working in close contact with desperately ill patients, getting the virus. Zoe didn't know what to do, or who to call to find out where Jean-Paul was or if he was sick.

"Do you have his parents' number?" her mother asked her.

"I do. But I don't want to worry them. Do you think I should call?" There was no other way to know, and it would put her mind to rest if they knew something reassuring that she didn't. Maybe he had called them. Or maybe his phone had died and he had no time to charge it, Darcy suggested.

It took Zoe an hour to get up the courage to call Jean-Paul's parents, and her hands were shaking when she did. His mother answered the phone, crying. Sobbing, she told Zoe that Jean-Paul had died two days before. He fell ill on the second day of his shift, and he died of cardiac arrest the day after. His parents didn't have Zoe's number to call her.

Zoe called her mother back, sobbing hysterically. "He's dead . . . oh my God, he died. He was twenty-six years old. I didn't even know he was dead. I just sat here, waiting." She couldn't stop crying, and Darcy couldn't even go to her to comfort her, because they might infect each other, if Darcy was incubating the virus and didn't know it, or if Zoe had contracted it from Jean-Paul, since he had obviously been incubating it. It was a cruel time for anyone who lost someone to the disease. You couldn't be there to bring them comfort in their final hours or hold them when they died or honor them properly after they did.

Darcy talked to her for a long time and knew that Jean-Paul's death would mark her forever. It was her first great love and might have led to marriage one day. After they hung up, Darcy sent texts to Charlie and Penny, to let them know, so they could reach out to support her. Charlie was shocked when he read the text, and showed it to Flavia.

"Oh no, the poor boy . . . so young . . ." she said, with tears in her eyes, mourning her father and now this young man whose life had been cut short so brutally while helping others. Charlie remembered that Jean-Paul was an only child and had been close to his parents. He could only imagine how they must feel now. And both were doctors and had been unable to try to save him, or even to be there when he died.

Penny called her sister the minute she saw her mother's text. She could feel vividly how terrible Zoe felt. They talked for hours that afternoon, and sometimes just sat in silence on the phone while Zoe cried and Penny wished that she could be there and hold her. They were closer to each other than to anyone on earth.

Darcy looked glum and was sitting quietly in their sitting room, staring into space, when Bill came home that night. He'd been out all day. He went out sometimes, and said he was required to go to the U.S. Embassy, but conditions there respected all the rules of social distancing, disinfecting, and confinement. He didn't say why he had to go. And he changed all his clothes and washed them when he returned, and they were given protective gear at the embassy, with masks and gloves. He was something of a mystery man, which was why Mme. Carton liked to theorize that he was a spy, which still made Darcy laugh when she thought about it. Darcy wasn't sure what a spy looked like, but very wholesome, serious, modest Bill Thompson was not her image of that at all. He occasionally quoted people at the American embassy or in French government as though he knew them personally, but that still didn't convince Darcy that he was a secret agent of some kind. He was just well connected through his job as an engineer.

He saw Darcy sitting alone in the sitting room off their bedrooms when he got back, and when she turned to look at him, she looked ravaged. He came toward her immediately and sat down near her. He hadn't had time to shower and change yet.

"Are you okay?" She shook her head. She'd been thinking of the last time she'd taken Zoe and Jean-Paul to dinner, at the bistro near the Belle Ville hotel. He was such a sweet boy, a really lovely young man, with a bright future ahead of him, and a wonderful girl who loved him. Zoe would have to pack up his things now, his medical books and clothes and all his mementos, and return them to his parents. No one should have to do that at nineteen, without even her mother to help her and console her.

She told Bill about Jean-Paul dying, and he was sad about it too. A great number of young people had died this time, and young children, and the elderly. She couldn't even go to comfort Zoe, because they all had to remain confined separately, and stay in the homes they were in, not mingle or visit, or have people over, whatever the reason.

Darcy noticed that Bill's hands were dirty and black with grease, as though he had been working on a car or doing manual labor. And he was wearing heavy work boots with his jeans that he hadn't worn before.

They talked about Jean-Paul for a long time, as Bill tried to comfort her. It was hard to find the words to do so. Nothing justified a twenty-six-year-old young man dying. They watched the news that night, which showed film clips of American soldiers and volunteers from the U.S. Embassy building field hospitals in the parking lots of two Paris hospitals, and she looked at Bill with a questioning glance, wondering if he had been one of them. Looking at the grease on his hands, it seemed possible. He made no comment, and she didn't dare ask. But she was beginning to think that Mme. Carton was partly right about him. Not a spy perhaps, but some kind of government agent or employee.

She called Zoe before she went to bed that night to make sure that she was all right. She sounded terrible, which was understandable, and Darcy convinced her to go to bed.

Mme. Carton was making her contribution to the medical workers' rescue work too. She had baked an enormous amount of cookies the day before, and had Bill deliver them to the Pitié- Salpétrière Hospital for the workers when he went out.

Darcy was collecting her recipes every time Mme. Carton made them a meal, which was lunch on most days and dinner every night. Darcy was actually learning to cook and would finish their confinement as a Cordon Bleu chef under the famous star's tutelage. Mme. Carton had shared with them one night during dinner that her own grandmother had died of the Spanish flu, shortly after her mother was born. She was a woman of many tales that she was willing to share about her life experiences, and Darcy loved spending time with her. She was a treasure chest of information, stories, people she had known, many of them famous, some not.

Darcy felt lucky to be spending the confinement with her. Sybille Carton had so much to teach on so many subjects, and without the confinement against the virus, Darcy would never have met her.

She said as much to Bill one day when they went for a walk with six feet between them, wearing masks and rubber gloves.


Zoe was still mourning Jean-Paul's death, and Darcy knew she would for a long time. Darcy had lost a male friend in college, not a boyfriend, but they had been friends, and had done hours of homework together. He died in a fire when he went to Florida for spring break and stayed in some terrible ramshackle house where the wiring caught fire and four young people had died. The Co 2-24 virus was like that. It burned lives and wasted them, and stole their futures from them.


After Mariette Nattier reorganized her factories, Philippe Nattier sat next to his wife's bed, as she coughed violently off and on for three days. Her fever rose until she was nearly delirious. He never left her for a minute. And on the fourth day, as he sat slumped over in a chair next to her bed, snoring, she woke and the fever had broken. She smiled as she looked at him, wondering why they had drifted so far apart for so long. When he woke up, he smiled when he saw her watching him and hugged her, and she tried to push him away.

"Don't! You'll catch it from me." She was sure she had the virus. She had all the symptoms.

"I don't care! You're alive. I was so afraid you wouldn't make it . . . I love you, Mariette." It had taken another world crisis to make them realize that they still loved each other.

"I love you too, Philippe. We've been such idiots for so long." She was crying when she said it, and he climbed into bed with her and held her in relief.

"I'm not letting you out of my sight again!" he said, holding her tight.

"I wouldn't want you to," she said shyly. It was like starting over from the beginning, which she would never have thought possible after so many years. But trauma and terror do strange things to people. For them, it had made the impossible become possible again, even desirable and worth whatever they had to do to get there. Living through a virus turned things around in ways they couldn't have imagined. They had lived separate lives for so long that they had forgotten why or how sweet it can be when you have someone you love next to you. Suddenly the world seems bright and new again. And their world had been transformed and was better than it ever had been. Mariette had gotten sick and survived it, which made Philippe realize how much he loved her, and the agony of loss hadn't touched them. They felt blessed as he nursed her through her recovery, and blessed again when, despite having nursed her so closely, he never caught it. The virus was completely unpredictable as to who it touched, and who it didn't. And it had touched them only in the best of ways, not as a curse, but a blessing.

# Chapter 10

The week after Jean-Paul died, Darcy got a frightening call from Zoe. She had offered to move in with her daughter, but Zoe had been exposed to the virus when Jean-Paul was incubating it, so it was too dangerous to stay with her, or even visit her.

Zoe was coughing when her mother answered the phone, and Darcy almost didn't recognize her voice when she spoke. She sounded like she had a bad cold or the flu, but her voice was weak and she said she had a fever. She had called one of Jean-Paul's medical school friends and he told her how sorry he was about Jean-Paul, and after that, all she did was cry. She finally managed to tell him her symptoms, and he said he was sure she had the virus, most probably caught from Jean-Paul. He advised her to stay home, and call the SAMU, the French equivalent of 911, if she felt dizzy or had trouble breathing or the fever went any higher. It was very high when she called him. She called her mother after that, and Darcy wanted to rush over to take care of her, but Zoe wouldn't let her.

"You can't! You'll get it, Mom. I won't let you in. I'm okay, I just feel lousy. I'll call the SAMU if I get worse, or go to the E.R. There's nothing they can do for it anyway." She was utterly miserable in body and mind. She cried all the time about Jean-Paul, and now every inch of her was aching. She said all she wanted to do was sleep. Bill Thompson found Darcy crying in their living room after she hung up.

"What's wrong?" he asked, coming to sit with her. From being together at every meal and spending evenings together, they were becoming friends and getting to know each other. He could already sense that she was a levelheaded woman, not given to tears or histrionics, so if she was crying, he was sure there was a good reason. Nearly everyone had a reason to cry these days, with so many people sick and dying.

"Zoe's sick, and she won't let me come over."

"Co 2-24 sick or something else?" he asked, as he instinctively reached out and took Darcy's hand in his. He'd never done that before, but she didn't mind. It was comforting to have some form of human contact.

"She must have the virus, since Jean-Paul did, and the incubation is about right. I don't want her in the apartment alone. She won't let me come and stay or even visit."

"She's right. She has to be in quarantine now. She can call the SAMU or go to a hospital if she gets too sick. There's nothing you can do for her, Darcy. You have to be sensible. And even in a hospital, they won't let you near her."

"I'm so sick of this whole thing!" she said, as she dabbed at her eyes with a handkerchief.

"We all are. It won't last forever. And she'll be okay. She's very young."

"So was Jean-Paul," she said miserably. And it wasn't fair. Poor Zoe had lost her first big love, and now she was sick herself, with no one to take care of her. "I let her stay in the apartment because I thought he'd be there to take care of her. Now she's alone, crying her heart out every day, and sick on top of it."

"You can FaceTime with her and keep track of her that way. You can call her every hour to check," he said, and Darcy laughed through her tears.

"She'll kill me if I do that," but it wasn't a bad idea to assess the situation herself on FaceTime.

"Maybe we can even set up a Zoom meeting with her and your daughter in Hong Kong. I'll help you do it." He tried to be encouraging and didn't quite know what to say. Not having children, it was hard for him to fathom Darcy's deep attachment to her twins as nearly adults, but he did understand that now that she and her husband would be divorcing, the twins were the only family she had, the only living relatives, since her parents had been gone for a long time. And beyond that, they were her babies and would always be children to her, at any age.

Bill could already tell how much her kids meant to her, and it was hard to reassure her convincingly since so many young people were dying too, many more so than with the coronavirus. This one had a hearty appetite for the young, who seemed to be in perfect health when they caught it and then died a few days later, as Jean-Paul had. But he had had a heavy dose of exposure, working in the hospital along with the medical staff. An extra strong dose, since he had spent two days at the desk in the ICU to relieve the nurses. There were so many calls from frantic families who couldn't be with their loved ones, that the phones in every hospital were ringing off the hook. Jean-Paul had manned the phones for two days and done other medical and nonmedical tasks in the hospital, and now he was dead. Darcy was beside herself thinking of the risk to Zoe from her exposure to him when he came home from his shifts.

"Why don't we go for a walk to get some exercise," Bill suggested gently, and she grabbed a jacket and followed him out. They stayed in the vicinity of the house in case they were stopped by the police and questioned about why they were out. They had to fill out a form each time they left the house, to the grocery store or pharmacy, or for a walk. Those were the only things they were allowed to do, and the police enforced it. They imposed fines if you were too far from home and didn't appear to be doing what the form said.

They walked a few blocks to the Seine and stood looking down at the river, standing the regulation six feet apart, but he was a comforting presence, even at a distance.

"What if she has to go to the hospital?" Darcy said after a long silence. "She won't have anyone with her." They weren't letting relatives in to see patients.

"You just have to believe that won't happen." He hoped that life wouldn't be that cruel to her, to lose her daughter. But there was no telling how far the epidemic would go, or who would suffer losses. He just hoped it wouldn't be Darcy. He had no family, no children, no deep attachments to anyone at the moment. If something happened to him, no one would mourn him. He would have been more than willing to sacrifice his own for a young life, but no one got to make those choices. All he could do was be there for Darcy, as best he could. She would have been deeply touched if she'd known what he was thinking.

They said very little on their walk, but it helped to get some air. She didn't call Zoe when they got back. She hoped that she was sleeping, trying to fight the fever. Her cough had sounded deep and ragged. Darcy went to her room when they got back to the house, and Bill closed his door softly. He had some calls to make.

Darcy was so upset she was going to skip dinner that night, but Mme. Carton wouldn't let her. Bill had told her about Zoe, and Mme. Carton asked for Darcy's help in the kitchen, saying she couldn't manage alone. She was making a gigot, a leg of lamb, that night and she said the pan was too heavy and she was afraid she'd drop it. So Darcy went upstairs to help her. Mme. Carton asked her to set the table. There were string beans with garlic, and mashed potatoes with truffles. And a paper-thin apple tart for dessert. The meal was superb. Bill loved it, and Darcy ate more than she expected to. She helped clean up the kitchen, and their landlady informed her that they were going to be working on chocolates and pastry that week, in Darcy's lessons in the kitchen. She had written out a whole program that afternoon after Bill told her, designed to keep Darcy busy until her daughter recovered. It was clever and well thought out, and she hoped it would help distract Darcy. Mme. Carton made a list of all her most challenging recipes that would be complicated to master and she intended to put Darcy through her paces. Darcy didn't even suspect the motive behind it, and was a little daunted when she heard the first few items on Madame's list, but she went along with it. It was a mission of mercy on the part of Sybille Carton.

Darcy had her blog to do too. So far, she had kept up to date with taking photographs of the neighborhood and reporting on confinement in Paris. Churches were closed and everything that involved commerce—restaurants, stores, any kind of gathering place—all the same things that had been closed before during the Covid-19 pandemic. The entire country and economy were on pause, as they were all around the world. People everywhere were worried about the world economy, but all Darcy could think of was her daughter.

She let Zoe call her so she didn't wake her, and for the first three days she continued to get worse, although her temperature stayed the same. She had a fever, but it wasn't as high as others she heard about who had the virus. Penny called her constantly too, wanting to know how Darcy thought her sister was doing, and checking how worried her mother was. Darcy tried to calm Penny's fears, and after two days Charlie called her to see what she knew, and what she thought. Zoe had FaceTimed with her father, and he thought she looked awful. Darcy answered his call immediately because Zoe was sick.

"Should she be in a hospital?" he asked Darcy.

"From what I've heard, she should if she gets any worse, but for now I think she's holding her own." Zoe still had enough to eat, although she wasn't hungry, and Darcy could see on FaceTime that she'd lost weight, but her cough was better. It was awkward talking to Charlie, but they kept the conversation focused on Zoe, and Darcy kept it as impersonal as possible. She didn't want to hear any more of his explanations or lame apologies. What was done was done, and it was over. She was angry now, finally, in a slow steady burn for what he'd done for two years, lying to her. All that remained between them now were their daughters. So she stuck with that as the only subject, and so did Charlie. She didn't ask him anything about his own life, or Flavia. She just said that she was glad he was well and staying in close confinement.

On the fourth day, Zoe said she felt better, and it took another two days for her to look it, although she was very thin and pale, and said she felt exhausted. A week after she had started to get sick, she was fever-free, her eyes looked bright again, she still had the cough but much less, and she looked like she had more energy as she walked around the apartment. She had slept through most of the week, and the rest of the time she was on the phone with either Darcy, her twin, or her father. She was definitely on the mend and had had a textbook case of the virus. But she had survived. Others, like Jean-Paul, hadn't been as lucky.

In the interim, Darcy had learned many of the intricacies of making French pastry, and the delicate art of making chocolates. She had made a *mousse au chocolat* that Bill said was the best he had ever tasted, and Mme. Carton gave it passing marks as well. Darcy had made a chestnut cake that was a masterpiece, and had had several lessons in sugar work, struggling to make it look like real flowers. Mme. Carton had kept her busy, and Zoe had lived. Bill and Sybille Carton had shaken hands over it in her kitchen when they were alone. Her little plan to distract Darcy had been a success.

He had been busy that week too. He was out very late several nights, and in the morning, Darcy had noticed his grease-stained blackened hands again, although he'd washed them several times. And coincidentally, American soldiers attached to the U.S. Embassy had built another field hospital in the Bois de Boulogne as their gift to the citizens and medical workers of Paris. Darcy wondered again if Bill had anything to do with the project, but he never mentioned it, nor did she.

Zoe was still tired but felt much better eight days after she'd gotten sick, when Penny called her in a panic, which was rare for her. She was normally the calmest person in the family, but she'd been on edge since Zoe had gotten sick. She couldn't live without her twin, and she sounded breathless when she called Zoe.

"What's up?" Zoe asked her. "You sound like someone shot you out of a cannon."

"I think they did. I just called Dad on his cell, and a woman answered. I thought I had the wrong number, but I asked for Dad anyway, just in case. She was perfectly civil. And she said he's in the hospital." Zoe's heart skipped a beat when Penny said it.

"Is he okay?"

"She said yes, and that it was more of a precaution. He has the virus."

"Did she say who she is?"

"No, and I was afraid to ask her," Penny said, still sounding shaken. "But she has his phone," which was an indication that they were close in some way.

"Do you suppose that's the problem between Mom and Dad? Do you think he has a girlfriend?" Zoe asked.

"I can't see Dad doing that, can you?" Penny said.

"No, but people do crazy shit sometimes, even parents. He's a good-looking guy for his age. A lot of women would want him," Zoe said, considering it.

"So does Mom," Penny added, "or at least she did, until she started sounding so pissed at him. Maybe he screwed up on a trip or something."

"Or did she sound like a secretary?" Zoe asked her.

"No, she didn't. She sounded very friendly and kind of sexy."

At nineteen, they could imagine his having a girlfriend and an affair, although it seemed unlikely to both of them, knowing their father. He was a very loyal person and they had never seen him flirt with other women. He wasn't that kind of man. Darcy had always believed that too, and discovered she was wrong.

"Did she tell you what hospital he's in?" Zoe asked her. "Can we call him?"

"I don't see how," Penny said. "Hospitals are jammed right now— patients' families are calling. And neither of us speaks Italian even if they do answer. The woman who answered said we could call her for updates, and she's sure he'll call us as soon as he gets out."

"Is she Dad's assistant in Rome?" Zoe asked, mystified.

"No, I talked to his assistant once. She had a heavy accent. The woman I talked to speaks good English. Not like us, but pretty close, with a British accent."

"Is she English?"

"No, it's that kind of Britishy accent some fancy Europeans have when they learn English from a British teacher or go to a fancy boarding school in Europe. Do you want to call and check her out?" Penny suggested, and Zoe shook her head. Zoe was bolder and would ask more questions.

"No, that's too weird, and she'd probably suspect we're in cahoots about her. She might tell Dad," which neither of them wanted, especially now if he was sick.

They each wanted to call their mother after they talked to each other, and both were curious about who the woman was who had their father's phone, and worried about his being in the hospital. Zoe was particularly anxious about his being sick, after what had happened to Jean-Paul.

After some discussion, Penny reluctantly agreed to be the one to tell her mother, since she had been the one who had talked to the mystery woman who had their father's phone. Zoe would only be reporting it secondhand, and she didn't want to be the one to tell her mother about another woman. She was well aware that Penny would handle it more diplomatically.

Darcy was finishing some things for the blog before dinner when Penny called her. It was midnight for her, in Hong Kong.

"Everything okay?" Penny usually went to bed early, unlike Zoe, who was a night owl.

"Yes, we're all fine," she reassured her mother. "I don't know if he told you, but I found out today, Dad's in the hospital in Rome. I talked to someone he left his phone with, and she said it's more of a precaution, but he has the virus. Did you know?" She was sure their mother would have told them if she did, and Darcy sounded as surprised as she had been.

"No, I didn't. That's awful. Did she say anything else?"

"No, just that I can call her for updates if I want to, and that she was sure he'd call me when he gets home. Do you know who she is?" Darcy was caught off-guard by the question and didn't know what to say for a minute.

"Not really," she said vaguely, "it must have been his assistant in Rome."

"It wasn't. I've talked to her before. This was someone else. She gave me the name of the hospital, I can give it to you." She did and Darcy jotted it down in haste. "I don't know why he didn't tell us," Penny said, concerned.

"I'm sure he didn't want to worry you."

"But he didn't call you either?"

"I'm certain he didn't want to scare us."

"And who is that woman? Why does she have his phone?"

"He probably can't have it at the hospital. Cellphones never work in hospitals anyway." Darcy felt like she was dancing in circles, avoiding Penny's questions. She had to remind herself too that she was no longer his wife, although she had been only weeks before. She had to learn new habits. He probably hadn't told her he was going to the hospital because he knew she was angry at him. And she could guess who the woman was. It was Flavia. But this was an awkward way for the girls to find out. Knowing how close they were, she could imagine that Penny had called Zoe first to tell her. They shared all information with each other.

"Can we call the hospital and try to find out how he is?" Penny asked, sounding suddenly very young and scared.

"Of course, I'll try, but they may be busy and I don't know if anyone will speak English. I'll let you know what I find out." She got off the phone as quickly as she could before Penny could ask any more questions about the woman who had their father's phone. And while Darcy called Italy, Penny called Zoe back.

"I don't think she knows anything either, about who the woman is. She was kind of vague about it, but I think she's just upset that Dad's in the hospital."

"Why wouldn't he call Mom before he went in?" Zoe asked suspiciously. "I think they're lying to us. Dad admitted that there's some kind of problem. Mom's not saying anything. Did she sound upset about some woman having his phone?"

"No. She acted like it didn't mean anything. She's trying to call the hospital now. She said she'd call if she finds something out."

"She won't. Hospitals are too busy right now." Zoe knew that from Jean-Paul. "And they probably don't speak English." They hung up a few minutes later, with the mystery unsolved as to who the woman was who had their father's cellphone, and the disturbing knowledge that he was in the hospital with the virus.

Darcy sat in her room thinking about it, after she made a futile attempt to call the hospital in Rome. She kept getting voicemails with messages in Italian. And since he didn't have his cellphone, she couldn't even send him a text to tell him she was thinking about him. As isolated as she was in Paris, he was just as much so in Rome, except that he had Flavia and her family to take care of him. She hoped he was going to be all right. It was a strange feeling that she had been his wife only weeks ago, and now suddenly, she was no one in his life.

She had a horrifying thought too that Charlie could die without ever telling the twins about Flavia. If that happened, they would never know that their parents were getting divorced, and it would fall to her to tell them they had an Italian half-sibling, and they would know that their father had cheated on their mother. It was a terrible legacy to leave them. Whatever happened, there was no escaping the truth now, whether he lived or died.

She hoped he would live for their daughters' sake, and the sake of his unborn child, who would be fatherless. And even though she was angry at him, as the man she had loved and been married to for twenty years, and the father of her children, she prayed that he would live.

## Chapter 11

The virus took over very quickly when Charlie came down with it. He was fine the night before, and woke up the next morning with a fever. He suspected immediately what it was, and Flavia called her doctor, who said to isolate him in a room, as far away as possible from her. He had to wear a mask and gloves, remain in the room with the door closed, not circulate in the house. Charlie was rigorous about it and moved to an unoccupied maid's room in the basement. It had its own bathroom, and he prayed he hadn't given it to Flavia during the incubation period, but sleeping in the same bed, living close together, he was terrified he had put her at risk. They had been careful not to see anyone else, so the only one who he could have exposed was Flavia. She was calmer than he was.

By that night, his fever was higher, and he had a bad cough. His body ached all over and all he wanted to do was sleep. She prepared food for him and left it outside the door, but she could see that he wasn't eating. He only ate a little soup, and the day after he was worse. Flavia called the doctor again, and Charlie reported he was short of breath, so they decided to send him to the hospital.

She called Roberto and told him, and he said he'd take him. Charlie didn't want to expose him, but he had no way to get there, so he bundled up with a scarf tied around his face in lieu of a mask and sat in the backseat of Roberto's car with the window open. He was wearing rubber gloves and didn't touch anything, and he left Roberto's car as quickly as he could and walked into the hospital under his own steam. Roberto was shocked at how bad he looked, the little he could see of him. As Charlie walked into the hospital, he was thinking of his daughters, and afraid he would never see them again. He would have texted them, but had left his phone with Flavia, who promised to speak to them if they called, and he was sure she would. He thought of calling Darcy, but it seemed pathetic to him. With everything he'd done, it seemed wrong to call her now, but he was deeply frightened that he would never see anyone he loved, even Flavia, and would never live to see their baby.

A sign directed him to where he was supposed to go to be examined and check in. As soon as he got there, they whisked him into an isolation room and took his temperature, which had climbed even higher. From then on, he was absorbed into hospital procedures and protocols, designed to protect others from contagion while treating his symptoms. He missed Flavia, but all he could do was hope he hadn't given it to her. It seemed like the Black Plague to him, or the Spanish flu, as he saws hordes of people arriving and being hustled into cubicles and small rooms, and there was a massive room with beds all lined up for those who had tested positive. There was almost something military about it, and the frightening thing about it was knowing that there were just as many people and more around the world in the throes of the same process, living the same risks, as sick as he was and worse, or losing loved ones the doctors couldn't save, some old, some young, men, women, children. It brought the word pandemic home to him as nothing else could. His real life and everything in it seemed totally remote now, and part of another world.

They gave him something for the fever, which brought it down a little. Most of the medical team that was treating him spoke some English, but many didn't. He had no idea what they were doing to him, and most of the time he didn't care. The hospital looked clean and modern, and the medical personnel wore what looked like spacesuits.

They gave him one of the medications they told him would diminish the symptoms, and on the sixth day of the illness, he felt better. Two days later, he woke up feeling like a human who had been badly beaten, but was at some level a human. He was too weak to talk, and his body felt ravaged. He could tell that he had lost a great deal of weight, and he wasn't sure what day it was.

He was in an enormous room full of beds in makeshift cubicles. It looked like it had been a cafeteria or a gym, an assembly room of some kind, and he had no idea how long he'd been there, or even how he'd gotten there. He vaguely remembered seeing Roberto, but after that all the memories of the past week were fuzzy. He didn't know if Flavia had been there or not, he couldn't remember. He was in the ward of people recovering from the disease. Those sicker than he were in the ICU. The ones who got better were discharged quickly, as soon as they were strong enough to leave. The hospital staff needed the beds, so they sent patients home as soon as it was medically safe and humanly possible. Charlie wanted to call Flavia to see how she was, but he couldn't find his cellphone anywhere, and it wasn't on the night table or in the drawer beneath it.

It was nighttime when he got someone to bring him a phone and plug it into the wall behind him. It rang and then he heard Flavia's gentle, husky voice and there were tears in his eyes as he just listened to it for an instant.

*"Pronto?"* she said. She didn't recognize the number, but had answered it anyway, in case it was the hospital. And deeply moved to hear her voice, he answered, as tears squeezed out the corners of his eyes as he lay there.

"Hello, beautiful, it's me . . . I'm still alive." It felt like the most important moment of his life, and the sweetest, just being able to talk to her. He felt like the whole room should stand up and cheer, and he along with them. They were all winners in that room, people who had survived it. The hardest was behind them.

"Oh my God, Charlie, are you okay? I've been so worried about you." She was laughing and crying all at once.

"I'm okay," his voice sounded like a croak. He hadn't spoken to anyone in days. "Did you get it?" He wanted to know immediately.

"No, I didn't. I'm fine. And Roberto hasn't gotten it either, from you or my father."

"Is your mom okay?"

"She's fine, but still very upset about my father. We all are. And I've been worried sick about you. I called the hospital but most of the time they didn't answer."

"Have my girls called?"

"Penny did. I told her you were in the hospital, and where. I haven't heard from them again. They probably called the hospital directly. From what I hear the hospitals are a madhouse. I told Penny you'd call when you get home." Flavia was so relieved to talk to him she was beaming. Her grief over her father had been obscured by her terror for Charlie. He was so sick when he left for the hospital. She had been able to get reports about him occasionally but not often, and they were allowing no visitors to the contagion ward. By their estimation, he would no longer be contagious in about three days. And he had had none of the heart problems or secondary complications that were typical of the worst cases. He had been lucky. "When can you come home?" she asked him.

"Soon . . . I don't know . . . in a few days, I think." His voice started to get weak after a few minutes, and he sounded exhausted. "I love you. I'll let you know when I'm coming home."

"Thank God." She sat there and cried again after they hung up, she was so relieved.

Charlie lay in his hospital bed smiling, as tears ran into his pillow. A minute later, he fell asleep.

Three days later, Charlie was strong enough to walk down the hall. He was no longer considered contagious, or a danger to anyone. He dressed in the clothes he had arrived in, and they hung on him. He looked haggard and pale, but he had survived. The hospital notified Flavia and Roberto, and Roberto came to pick him up. Flavia was waiting at home. They were still confined.

Roberto threw his arms around Charlie when he saw him, and he was so weak Roberto almost knocked him down. Charlie was smiling, and so happy to leave the hospital. They had taken good care of him, although he didn't remember a great deal of it. They had been professional and dedicated, working tirelessly for long shifts. Many of the hospital staff had caught the virus and become patients themselves. The same was true around the world.

It was a short drive to Flavia's house, and Roberto brought him up-to-date on family news for the last ten days. They were all still shaken about Umberto, but they had been worried about Charlie too.

Roberto walked him into the house with an arm around him to steady him, and Flavia tried not to show it, but she was shocked when she saw him. He said he guessed he had lost about ten pounds, but it looked more like twenty.

Charlie sat down on the couch as soon as he walked in and glanced around, grateful to be back, and to be alive. Flavia looked more beautiful than ever in a starched white shirt and jeans. She was four months pregnant now, and the baby was fine. She'd been to the doctor a few days before. She had been so desperately afraid that she would lose Charlie. It was all she could think about for the past eleven days. He had to build up his strength now and gain back some weight. But for him, the worst was over. For so many others, it wasn't, and the death toll had been higher than predicted. Not as high as Covid-19, but Co 2-24 had claimed many victims. It had been kinder to Italy this time, but other countries hadn't fared as well. The countries that had learned their lesson the last time took it more seriously this time, and had done better than others. Those who had ordered confinement immediately had suffered the least loss of life.

Roberto left them a few minutes later, and Flavia sat down next to Charlie, and held him in her arms.

"I'm so sorry I couldn't be in the hospital with you."

"I wouldn't have let you." He felt her belly under the shirt and smiled to find it had grown bigger just in a short time. "He's growing." He smiled proudly and she nodded. "I want to call the girls," he said quietly. She went to get his cellphone and handed it to him.

He was stunned to realize that it actually took a physical effort to make the call. Every movement and gesture was an effort now. They had told him in the hospital to rest and work on getting his strength back before he tried to be too active, and now he could see why. He felt as though he had been sick for six months and not two weeks.

He called Penny first, and she shouted with excitement when she heard him. "Dad! Are you okay?"

"I'm fine. I'm sorry I couldn't call you. It was complicated from the hospital, and I didn't have my phone."

"I know, I talked to your friend, and Mom's been getting reports from the hospital whenever she could get through and find someone who spoke English. When did you get out?"

"About half an hour ago," he said, and felt stronger just listening to his daughter. Being in the hospital, fighting for his life, he had felt as though everything he had ever loved and held dear had disappeared, even Flavia, and his daughters. "It feels so great to be up and out again."

"Was it really awful, Dad?" He paused, trying to decide what to say, and then opted for the truth.

"It was, and scary as hell. I thought I was going to die." Penny had tears in her eyes listening to him. "But I was lucky, I didn't. And the world will be out of this mess eventually, and we'll move forward. How are you doing in Hong Kong?"

"We're bored and tired of being in lockdown too. I hope we can go home soon."

"So do I."

"Are you going to go back to New York now, Dad?"

"I need to get my strength back first. I'm going to stay in lockdown here until things calm down in New York." He wasn't in a hurry to go back, he wanted to stay in Rome with Flavia, but he didn't say that to Penny. "I'll call you again soon, sweetheart. I just wanted you to know that I'm fine and out of the hospital, and I'm sorry I couldn't talk to you from there."

"It's okay. You sound great, Dad. Talk to you soon." They hung up, and he called Zoe next, while Flavia was putting something together in the kitchen.

Zoe was just as excited to hear him, although she still sounded subdued, after losing Jean-Paul. They talked about her having had the virus too, but a much milder version. They agreed on how nasty it was, and he only gently touched on her sadness about Jean-Paul. "Are you doing okay?"

"Yeah. It's hard," she admitted, and she wasn't referring to the confinement. "I get really sad sometimes. I miss him so much."

"I know, baby. Losing someone you love is hard." He thought of Darcy when he said it. He did miss her at times, but he also knew that he couldn't go back there, and didn't want to. He knew he had made the right choice staying with Flavia, and not trying to piece things back together with Darcy. It would never have worked, and hadn't in a long time, or his double life would never have happened. He was sad to see a big part of his life end. It had been good for a long time, but Flavia was the woman and the life he wanted now.

"Have you talked to Mom yet?" Zoe asked him.

"I was going to call now to let her know that I'm out and I'm okay. I called you and Penny first."

"She was worried about you too. We all were."

"Thank you. I'm okay now, I just have to get my strength back. Be careful in Paris, Zoe."

"I am, Dad." She sounded sad. It was hard being in the apartment without Jean-Paul. Everything reminded her of him, his books and his belongings were everywhere, and his clothes in the closet. His parents weren't going to come for his things until after the confinement ended. She felt like she was living with his ghost. Charlie could sense that and was sorry for her when they hung up.

Flavia came to get him then. She had set a beautiful lunch table to welcome him home. There were linen placemats embroidered with yellow flowers, with matching napkins. There was roast chicken and a salad, spinach pasta primavera, and a vase of yellow flowers on the table.

"Welcome home," she said softly, and he kissed her. As he did, he remembered all the times he had thought of her in the hospital, when he thought he was dying and would never see her again, and never know their baby. Being back with her was like a rebirth, returning from the grave. She was a dream come true for him, and he had just been through the worst nightmare of his life. She was the rainbow after the storm.

They sat down and enjoyed their lunch together. After lunch, they went to bed and had a nap. It was the perfect homecoming, to the love of his life.

When he got into bed, he sent Darcy a text in Paris. "Thank you for checking on me. Got out of the hospital this morning. On the mend. Hope all is well in Paris. See you when we're all back in New York. Take care, C." He didn't sign it "love" because he didn't want to mislead her. He loved her as the mother of his children and a cherished memory, but she wasn't the woman in his life anymore. Things were different now. Darcy knew it even before she read his text. She was relieved that he had texted her and hadn't called. She was glad he was alive, but she didn't want to hear his voice.

Reality was waiting for Charlie when he got back from the hospital. All four of his stores were hard hit by this second pandemic. They had to close along with everyone else. Their online shopping feature had never been strong, and their customers weren't used to buying from them in that format. They'd always made a big point of coming to their stores. Now they were closed and they had an enormous payroll to carry and no income to balance it. In less than four weeks, they had lost millions, and they had paid for their fall orders in advance in Milan. They hadn't ordered in Paris, since fashion week had been canceled, but they had done a huge buy at fashion week in New York. They had a deficit that looked like the national debt. Charlie read the reports from his accounting department. The last time this had happened, four years before in the Covid-19 pandemic, their faithful Chinese investors had bailed them out. This time, they were suffering from a second hit, and their Hong Kong investors regretfully informed them that they were pulling out, which made the situation even more disastrous.

Charlie talked to Roberto about it on the phone. He didn't want to risk Flavia's safety by having him to the house. Charlie was no longer a danger to her, since he wasn't contagious now, but Roberto still could be. Charlie wasn't taking any chances with her.

"Economically, this is a much tougher situation for us than the last one. Without my Hong Kong guys, I'm out of business. A lot of corporations that came through the last one are precarious now. They're going to go down like ninepins without someone to save them."

"What are you going to do?" Roberto asked. Tedesco was taking a hit too, but their outlay wasn't as big, and the Italian government had already committed to helping them. The U.S. government wasn't going to shore up Charlie's stores.

"We may have to close our doors for good and declare bankruptcy. That'll be a first for me. But I've made a fortune before, I can do it again. Times will get better, but not fast enough for me to save the stores. The concept of a department store is antiquated," he admitted. "The boys in Hong Kong know that. It's the online fashion merchants who are making all the money now. I never wanted to do that at Gray's, it wasn't our concept. But if I start again, that's the direction I would go, without a store. It would keep our overhead down." Charlie was already planning ahead. "By the time I get back to New York, I'll know if we can bring the stores back to life, or if they're dead for good." He sounded serious but not panicked, and Roberto admired the calm, businesslike way he looked at it, and his plan of action if they had to give up the stores.

"Maybe we can do something together," Roberto said, thinking about it. "Let's keep the communication open on that." Roberto liked the idea of a strong online presence too, which Tedesco didn't have either. Umberto had been vehemently opposed to it. It wasn't of his generation. It wasn't really of Charlie's either, but he was forward-thinking and had an open mind, and was a brilliant businessman. He was staying vigilant and as undisturbed as was possible in the current economic storm, which was inevitable after a pandemic, even if it was smaller than the previous one. But this was economically more dangerous, because the economy had only just gotten back on its feet after the first one.

He was advising Flavia about her business too. She had similar concerns, but on a smaller scale. Charlie made some excellent suggestions, which would help her hang onto her business. And she qualified for government help too. Charlie advised her to apply for it immediately. She followed his advice unquestioningly, and knew he was right. Roberto and the others were impressed by the suggestions he made. He was one of them now and spent as much time advising them for their brands as he did working on his own affairs. The Tedescos, especially Flavia, were proud and grateful for his help. As the days went by, he was less and less optimistic about his own stores.

While Charlie and the Tedescos made plans to salvage their businesses and began to think of new endeavors better adapted to today's world, the pandemic continued to blaze its way through every country, killing some people, injuring others, and sparing some. As he recovered from the virus, Charlie was shocked by how hard it had hit him, and it was hitting the world economies just as hard. Charlie was preparing for it, and bracing himself for what he saw was a rapid and inevitable fall. After the virus, it would be the governments and economies and banks that would be weakened, many of which would collapse. And then there would be a time of enormous growth when they rebuilt. Being part of that rebirth and renewal was his plan.

# Chapter 12

In Paris, as in other cities, people were getting tired of the relentless lockdown, while the population continued to get sick. It was hard not to be discouraged, while friends and loved ones fell ill or died. Others survived the virus. The contagion was acute, and yet it hopscotched around people, sometimes killing a whole group, or most or all of a family. Watching the news and reading the papers only created more angst.

Darcy's cooking lessons with Mme. Carton continued. Darcy had a whole stack of her recipes now, carefully written out and put in a binder. Darcy's cooking skills had improved remarkably, and she was enjoying it now.

She talked to her daughters several times a day. Both girls were finishing up their semester online, with papers due for credit, which were even more important now since there were no lectures or classroom work. Penny's grades had held up despite the confinement. Zoe's were good, but she had a harder time concentrating after losing Jean-Paul. Being in Paris was as traumatic as being in every other big city at the moment. The numbers of deaths and newly sick people every day were still high. They were slowly coming down, but not fast enough, and everyone feared being confined for longer, as had happened in the last pandemic. It had gone on for months. And no one was sure where this one was headed. It had begun to look much more ominous than originally predicted. A shocking number of people had had the virus.

Other than Mme. Carton's cooking lessons, what Darcy was enjoying most in Paris were the quiet evenings with Bill in their little sitting room after dinner.

They talked about a million different subjects, books they both liked, music, places where they had traveled, her children, his favorite pastimes, Annapolis, his life in the Marines when he was very young, and his transition to his "nomadic life" after his wife died.

"Do you still miss her?" she asked him one night. There was a sadness in his eyes which she had come to recognize. He kept things to himself a lot, and was generally very guarded, but sometimes when he spoke to Darcy, he let his guard down, and she could see into his soul.

"Sometimes," he said honestly, "I wonder what we would have been like as a couple if she had lived. She died so long ago, we were barely more than kids, we were in our twenties. It's not so easy to make a marriage work twenty years later as grown-ups. Maybe it wouldn't have worked by now, like you and Charlie." He knew a lot about her life now, and her values. He knew most of it.

"I thought Charlie and I had it made in the beginning. I was sure it would last forever. I never thought it would end like this, in a divorce, with him with another woman and a baby. I never saw that one coming."

"Most people don't," Bill said gently. She could sense that he was powerful and decisive, and he had strong opinions, but he had a kind, empathetic side to him that she was coming to respect deeply. She loved talking to him. He had been comforting and helpful for all four weeks of the confinement.

"What are you going to do when this is over?" she asked him one night.

"Wait for another assignment, probably in the Middle East or Asia."

"You don't get tired of that? Living in a tent for two years?"

He smiled. "I get very tired of it sometimes, but it's what I do, and it's interesting. Everything's a mess when I get there, in some godforsaken area that's been through a war or a disaster of some kind. And little by little you clean it up and make it better than it was before. They need me so the roofs don't fall in and the bridges don't collapse after I leave. I enjoy it because I can see the difference I've made by the time I go. In some jobs, you can't do that." It reminded her of something when he said that, and she decided to ask the question.

"Did you have anything to do with the field hospitals the Americans donated that they put up here?" He smiled again when she asked.

"I might have. Same deal. So the tents don't collapse when we leave. I have friends at the embassy and I offered to give them a hand when I heard about the project. I was happy to help."

"That's very impressive," she said, looking at him with admiration. "It must be a good feeling to know you're helping people. I always thought engineering was just technical, but the way you do it, it has a very human side. Those field hospitals looked amazing." She had only seen them on TV during the lockdown.

"We got each one up in five days. We had a lot of people helping us. The French army gave us a hand too. We showed them how to do it, so they could do it without us next time. The American government donated all the materials, and the labor. In a situation like this, everyone has to work together."

"It makes what I do seem so frivolous and insignificant," she said.

"It isn't. I've been reading your blog. You're educating people, showing them things they'd never see otherwise. You're teaching them, entertaining them, broadening their experience. I like that. My work is all nuts and bolts and mechanical."

"Not exactly. You saved lives with the field hospitals."

"I'm just the guy on the ground who makes it happen. The medical personnel are the ones who save lives. It's all about teamwork. That's what I loved in the Marines. Everybody works together. When it goes right, all the pieces fit and then it all makes sense. I enjoyed working on the hospitals. We built one on the project I was on in Saudi Arabia. The ones here were easier. I built some in Iraq too. It's easier and you get more done when no one's shooting at you," he said with a grin. There were times when he amazed her, and he was so easygoing and unassuming. Charlie was much more flamboyant, although he had his merits too. But Bill suited her better, and being with him was more peaceful.

"What are you going to do when you go home?" he asked her the same question, and she thought about it.

"Find a lawyer and get divorced, for one thing. I guess that will be a mess for a while. Figuring out who gets what. I don't know how that works yet. At least the girls aren't little kids anymore, that would be harder. They're off to their own skies. And then I'll make the same rounds I always do, fashion week in three or four cities twice a year, discovering new products, or theories, medical news, or inventions. I guess there will be information about the pandemics for a long time. And I'll talk about whatever social changes and new information come out of all this. We still have a lot to learn about how it happened." He nodded agreement.

He always made their evenings interesting, and she had started to realize that when the lockdown was over and they went back to their normal lives, she was going to miss him. He had been very careful about not starting anything romantic with her. She could have been attracted to him, but he had walls up and she sensed that he didn't want to go there. Getting involved didn't fit with the life of a nomad. And he truly was one. He loved talking to her, and knowing that she'd be there when he got back from whatever meeting or project he was currently involved with, but the life he led didn't leave room for a woman. He had tried it a few times, and everyone just got hurt in the end when he moved on. So he was no longer willing to try.

The numbers finally started to come down significantly, the projected peaks were reached, fewer people were getting sick and fewer died. They weren't down to Ground Zero yet, but they were getting there faster than the experts had estimated. The rapid lockdown, especially simultaneously all over Europe and the United States, did exactly what they hoped it would. The new pandemic ended as rapidly as it had started. It had taken far fewer lives than the last one. But nonetheless, in six weeks, it had taken healthy young people, the predictable frail older ones—though many of them had survived—and even some children. This time it had been brief compared to the last one, just as everyone had hoped.

It wasn't completely over after six weeks, but it was almost there, enough to let people venture out of their homes with caution, wearing masks and gloves. The scientists knew that cases would still crop up here and there, but for the most part, it was over, like a war that had been won, and the truce had been signed. There were always a few die-hard snipers left in those cases who came out of caves to claim a final victim, but the enemy had been stopped. The dragon was on a leash now and would not be allowed to roam free again. He had come to kill them, with his tail brandishing, and his ferocious claws and teeth, and had run out of steam.

The survivors straggled out from where they had been hiding. And some who had been exposed to the virus never got it and survived, which was a relief. A broad spectrum of people had come through it. Flavia was healthy and blossoming, and Charlie had nearly died. They had both been exposed to the same people at the same time. Flavia's mother had been untouched and they had lost Umberto. An aunt and some remote cousins had been lost. Philippe Nattier never caught it from Mariette. Zoe had a mild case and Jean-Paul had died. Penny and her roommates were safe in Hong Kong and none of them got it. Bill Thompson was untouched. Sybille Carton was better than ever at eighty-four. And so many had contributed to the war effort to harness the disease and stop it.

The Nattiers were going to get a commendation from the President for redirecting their factories' production for the national good.

Once confinement was over, Darcy began making plans. Zoe had a chance to see her friends again and spent time with them. She was able to mourn Jean-Paul with them. She helped his parents pack up his things and got her own ready to send home. Penny was wrapping things up in Hong Kong. The virus had been short-term in retrospect, and so completely gone that there were very few restrictions left, except for some social distancing, and still a lot of hand-washing. Many people still wore masks when they went out, although they'd been told it wasn't necessary. The enemy was gone.

Co 2-24 was shorter than Covid-19, but it took a lot of businesses with it nonetheless. It was the second big economic hit in four years, and the second wave had been more destructive. By the time it was truly over, Charlie knew he had lost all four stores and had to declare them bankrupt. But in spite of the losses, Paris was reviving slowly, and every day of freedom after the lockdown felt like a gift.

Bill invited Darcy to dinner at one of his favorite restaurants, which was hers as well. Victims of the virus had lost a shocking amount of weight. Others, who hadn't gotten it, had eaten too much while confined and gained, without the ability to exercise enough. Darcy could see plainly the effect of the stress she'd been under, between her lost marriage at the beginning, Zoe catching the virus, Jean-Paul's death, and the constant ongoing strain of living in uncertainty and being confined. It felt strange now that it was over to be able to go out and do whatever you wanted. She was looking forward to dinner with Bill while she was making her exit plans. The airlines were taking off again, trains were functioning. Some people were still hesitant about going out, while others exploded in celebration as soon as they were allowed.

They were liberated in April, and it was fully spring by then. The school semester for both Zoe and Penny ended in May. Darcy was planning to leave Paris then.

She thoroughly enjoyed her celebratory dinner with Bill. It felt strange to be wearing nicer clothes again, to look chic, wear makeup, get hair and nails done, and put on high heels. It was startling how much difference it made for one's spirits and how hard it had been to function in wartime mode day after day for six weeks, as though waiting for bombs to fall in a war. It had been a war, and there had been heroes, mostly all the medical workers who had saved lives. The damage would have been far worse without them, and many of them had died.

When Bill took Darcy to dinner, she was planning to stay for another three or four weeks, while Zoe took her final exams and turned in term papers, which would give her credit for the year. And Penny was doing the same in Hong Kong. Zoe wanted Charlie to come and visit them in Paris, but the frontiers were only just opening up, plane schedules between countries weren't fully regular yet, and he told her he was too busy and would see her at home when they all returned. She was busy enough herself with school and friends that she didn't object too vehemently. She and her mother had gotten together as soon as they were freed from confinement. Darcy had rushed over to see her the moment it was announced, and Zoe fell sobbing into her arms. She had been through a lot for a nineteen-year-old girl, with Jean-Paul's death and her own illness. But it had been a comfort knowing that at least her mother was nearby.

Penny hadn't had that in Hong Kong, which had forced her to grow up too, to be frightened and anxious for so long, so far from home. Charlie was speaking to both girls frequently, but he hadn't told them about Flavia yet. He wanted to do it face-to-face in New York. He felt he owed them that, and he had to settle his business dealings, and finalize the divorce settlement with Darcy. She had only spoken to him once briefly since she'd seen him in Rome, but she was grateful that he had survived the virus, that the twins still had a father.

People weren't talking about the virus now, they were talking about the economy, in every country, and how to bring it back to life. With the second pandemic ending faster than the first one, there was hope that the world economy would take off again sooner than the doomsayers had feared. There had been a lot of them, rumormongers who dashed people's spirits while everyone struggled to hang on. And there were some who embraced conspiracy theories to terrify everyone needlessly.

"How do you think it will affect your consulting business?" Darcy asked Bill at their celebratory dinner. He had insisted on ordering champagne, which seemed appropriate. He toasted her and thanked her for the many evenings they had spent together.

"You kept me going every time I started to lose hope," he admitted to her.

"You did the same for me," and there had been some very hard times, after seeing Charlie in Rome, and being separated from both her daughters for the entire confinement. She had never been away from her children for as long in their entire lives.

"I have a confession to make, Darcy. I thought about telling you before, but I decided it would be better after we were out of confinement."

"You have a wife and ten children." She smiled at him.

"No, only nine," he teased her. "It's about my consulting job," he said, lowering his voice so only she could hear him. "That does describe it, though not completely. There are some additional components to it." She listened carefully. In some ways, he had remained a mystery, although they had gotten to know each other well. But not quite as well as she thought. He wanted to adjust that now, at what felt like the right time. "I am a consultant, and an engineer. But I work for the government, not a consulting agency, although I suppose you could call it that. I'm a senior agent of the CIA." She looked at him for a minute and started to laugh, as all the puzzle pieces that hadn't fit before slipped into place.

"Mme. Carton said you were a spy. So she wasn't that far off after all."

"I'm not a spy, just an agent," he said modestly. "And I was returning from a two-year mission when this whole mess began." Now that he said it, she wasn't surprised. It all made sense, and gave substance to his "nomadic" life, as he called it.

"And where are you going now?" she asked. What he had told her was intriguing. And it suited him.

"I haven't been assigned yet. They want me here for a while. We have to dismantle the field hospitals and take care of some other things. There are several medical task forces gathering information.

There's a lot of cleaning up to do after something like this. I'll probably go back to the States about a month after you do, in June. Maybe a little longer, depending on how it plays out. They may reassign me from here, or send me back to Washington for a while. I have an office in the Pentagon that I haven't seen in two years." He looked relaxed talking to her about it. He knew the information was safe with her. "I can't do this forever, but it works for now. It's a special kind of life. It made sense when I lost my wife. I didn't want to get tied down anywhere, and then it became a way of life. I'll probably retire sometime in the next five years and do something else, if I can figure out what. I'm turning fifty this year. I figure another five and I'll be done. A lot of agents leave around the age I am now and start other lines of work, but I love what I do. It doesn't leave much room for other people in your life. It's been ideal for me, since I'm not married, have no family left, and don't have kids. I'm the guy they want, because they can send me anywhere. And it's an interesting life, being on the front lines."

"And a dangerous one, I suspect," she said, and she could see easily now why there was no woman in his life. There was no place for one with his kind of job and the way he lived.

"This last month has given me a taste for a different kind of life again," he said cautiously, "that and Mme. Carton's food, and talking to you," he said, with a question in his eyes. She wasn't sure what he was asking her, or even if he was. What he had revealed to her was more of a statement than a question. He had finally told her who he was. Until then, there had always been a part of him that he held back. He had been holding back for twenty years and staying unattached on purpose. It was the only way to do the job he did and do it well. She wondered if he could ever leave that life. It seemed unlikely. What he did was so much more interesting and exciting than anything else would be after the CIA. Mme. Carton had not been far off the mark with her assessment. She was a wise woman and had recognized the signs in him. "I'm glad you didn't get sick, Darcy. Or Mme. Carton. I was scared to death you would."

"We were lucky, you too," she said softly.

"And careful. It was vital that we followed the rules. That's what ended this one faster than the last one. The spread had to be stopped early, and it was. It's damn hard to confine a whole country. But everyone did it right this time."

"It feels amazing to be out again, doesn't it?"

"I love being out with you," he said, looking relaxed, "although our little sitting room at Sybille's house feels like home now. I'm going to miss it. And you. They'll probably send me to some god-awful backwater now to make up for it, so I don't go soft on them. I'll remember all those nights when we sat and talked, when I'm on some mission in a place no one's ever heard of." She had a glimpse now into what a lonely life he led, and she felt sorry for him. It was an exciting job, and even an important one most likely, but not an easy way to live. You had to sacrifice everything to do it. "And what happens when you go back?" he asked her.

"I've got to work out the divorce with Charlie, get the girls settled after all this. We'll spend some time in the Hamptons before the girls go back to Boston in September, and then I'll see. Maybe Paris Fashion Week in September. I want to come back here and visit Sybille. I have a project I want to do first." He nodded, wishing he'd be there too, but by then he'd be long gone, halfway around the world. The countries that he specialized in were not places she was likely to visit, nor would he want her to. They sent him to troubled areas most often, and he loved the challenge and didn't mind the risks. But he would never risk her.

"I'd like to visit you when I come back to the States, before I take off again. I never know how long I'll be gone, usually one or two years, sometimes longer." It made her sad to think of him on the road alone, in his dangerous, lonely life, and not seeing him for that long.

"I'd love to see you," she said simply. "You'll have all my details when I go. I'm easy to find."

"I'd love to see your girls too." He had met Zoe briefly when she stopped by to see her mother, on her way to class. "I'd like to meet Penny."

"She's flying home when we are. And Charlie has to come and tell them his news."

"That won't be easy for them," he said.

"No, it won't. A divorce, a stepmother, and a new baby brother or sister all at once. I'd met Flavia before, several years ago. People say she's a nice woman, but that's a lot for her to take on too. I don't envy her, although I love my girls. Zoe is liable to give her a run for her money." She smiled at the thought, and he laughed.

"I think that's why I lead the life I do," he said, smiling. "Women can be complicated, even at their age. That's not my skill set, teenage girls."

"They're pretty grown-up now. A few years ago, they would have been harder. What they won't like is that he's been lying to us for two years. That won't sit well with them. They're very principled and very black-and-white about right and wrong. I feel that way about it too, in his case. Things happen, people change, but the biggest mistake he made was not owning up to it sooner. Anyway, it is what it is. They'll get through it, and they'll forgive him. They should, he's their father, and he loves them, even if he made a mess of this." Bill loved how reasonable she was, how compassionate and forgiving. He had been noticing it for the last month and a half as he got to know her.

They went for a walk after they left the restaurant and wound up in front of Notre-Dame, all lit up. The structural repairs were still under way, but due to be finished any day. There had been considerable progress. It was magical being there, and Darcy appreciated being in the open air, free to move around again. The evening with Bill had been wonderful.

They walked back to the Carton house, and took their time, savoring every moment of freedom. Darcy knew she would never take that for granted again. She had thoroughly enjoyed the evening with Bill and his revelations, and she didn't take him for granted either. He was a special person with an unusual job and a remarkable life. She was happy to be going home in a few weeks, but she was going to miss him, now more than ever. After his confessions, he was a whole person to her, and even more to miss.

# Chapter 13

The final days in Paris flew by, getting everything organized. Darcy had been in Paris for almost three months by then, and was surprised by all the papers, reports, magazines, trinkets, and odds and ends she had managed to collect in her room at Mme. Carton's house. A lot of it she threw away, and some of it she kept and shipped home.

She took Mme. Carton to lunch at the Espadon at the Ritz before she left. They both agreed her cooking was better, but it was fun to get dressed up and go out. Every outing was a special treat now, every sunny, warm May day felt like a little piece of heaven. Zoe was busy saying goodbye to her friends and turning in her last papers, so Darcy was on her own for her final days, and even though she'd been trapped there for nearly three months, she was enjoying the time in Paris. It had never looked prettier, or more welcoming. Darcy spent hours walking to her favorite places. They were giving up Zoe's apartment when they left, so she had packing to do there too.

Bill took Darcy to their favorite restaurant again. He had been busy since the end of the confinement and was out every day until dinnertime. He still had dinner with Darcy and Mme. Carton almost every night. And now that Darcy knew what his job really was, he told her that he was working out of the U.S. Embassy, where they had given him a temporary office. He hadn't been reassigned yet, and expected to hear every day, but so far he hadn't. They would be sending him to Washington before he left for the new assignment, to be briefed on the politics of the new location, and his mission there. He was going to visit Darcy in New York after he got to Washington.

In the meantime, he was overseeing the dismantling of the field hospitals. They took longer to take down than they had to put up, and special fumigation teams came in to disinfect them. It was like putting out the last embers of a fire that had nearly devoured the world.

One still saw people wearing masks in the street, but it was the last remaining sign of Co 2-24, and there were very few people who still wore them. It was as though the virus had gone out on the tide and disappeared. There were no new cases reported in France, and there hadn't been for a month. The city and the country were safe again, as well as all of Europe. The U.S. had returned to normal, and Asia, Africa, and India were clear too. Like a demon that had returned to hell, the virus had vanished. And it had left an aura of benevolence in its wake. People were kinder to each other, smiled at each other in the street, helped older people carry packages. They chatted with each other while waiting for buses. It was as though they had survived a war together, and there was a new solidarity among them. Traffic seemed more civilized, there were no horns blaring, strangers greeted each other. People looked happy just to be walking down the street.

Darcy was almost sorry to leave, although she was excited to go home too. There had been so many nights when she had wondered if she would ever see her home again, or be with her children.

She had lost Charlie since she'd come to Europe to surprise him, but as it turned out she had lost him long before and just hadn't known it.

She wasn't looking forward to seeing him when he came back to New York, but they had to go through all the mechanics and legalities of the divorce now. It wasn't going to be pleasant but it had to be done, just to get everything in order. He had his own problems to solve with the bankruptcy of his stores. She was sad to see them disappear. They had been beautiful, and she had always enjoyed them. But they had suddenly become part of another era, and no longer made sense. Zoe said he was planning to start a new business with someone in Italy, the brother of a friend. She guessed that it was Flavia's brother, so she knew he was busy. He wanted to get to New York by the end of May, so she and the twins would have a couple of weeks to settle in before he arrived. She was planning to go to the Hamptons with the girls for July and August. She was looking forward to it, and having the summer together before they went back to school. As she always did, Darcy had organized everything before they even got home. The townhouse had been closed for months, and their housekeeper had been confined in Brooklyn, but she was back on the job now getting everything ready for their return, scrubbing the house until it gleamed.

Her last dinner with Bill had a bittersweet quality to it. She was sad to leave him, and he was sad to see her go, even though he'd see her in New York sometime in the next month. The bond that they shared now, after living under the same roof in confinement for nearly three months, was a strong one. Nothing would ever take those memories away, or the time they had shared. They were comrades of war.

They walked home from the restaurant, savoring their last evening together. Darcy realized that it would never be the same again between them. He would disappear on his mission. And she would have to adjust to her new life, alone.

"The house is going to seem empty without you tomorrow, Darcy," he said sadly. "I won't have you to talk to when I get home from work, or after dinner." They had both grown fond of Sybille Carton, and Darcy loved to prod her into telling her stories of the famous actors she'd worked with, and the films that she'd made, and the men she'd been in love with before she married. Her memories had lent spice and charm to their confinement, but she was more fun in a group than one on one.

When they got back to the house, Bill saw that Darcy's bags were packed and already in the hallway, and he looked at her with a serious expression.

"If I led a different kind of life, things would be different between us, or I'd like them to be. I made a decision a long time ago, when I chose this life, that I don't have a right to inflict it on someone else. It wouldn't be right. You might not see me for a year, or even two sometimes. It's a choice one has to make. And I did. You deserve so much more than that, or what I could give you."

"I know," she said softly. "You deserve more than that too."

"When Jeanie died, it felt like the right choice for me twenty years ago. And now it's late in the day, at nearly fifty. This is the only life I know. It's familiar and easy for me." It didn't sound easy to her. They had been attracted to each other since the beginning, but had never acted on it. With the anxiety and pressure of their confinement, it had seemed like too much to take on, to both of them. But now they were free again, and he was going to be sent on a dangerous mission some-where in the world where she couldn't go with him, and he might never return. He lived a life of danger and sacrifice. She wished it were otherwise, but it wasn't. It was who he was now, and she accepted that about him. They had been brought together by unusual circumstances and now he was going back to his life, and she to hers, or what was left of it after the divorce. He kissed her gently on the cheek, and it took every ounce of strength to go to his own room that night, and watch her door close, knowing she was still there for one more night.

She lay in bed all night, thinking about him, wanting to go to him and ask him not to go back to that life, but she had no right to do that. And he didn't want to turn back and lose someone he loved again one day. It had almost killed him the first time, and he couldn't risk it again. With no partner, and no attachments, he couldn't lose someone he loved.

She was up and dressed in the morning when he came out of his room in the U.S. navy jumpsuit he was wearing for work. The navy owned the tents they were dismantling.

They had breakfast in the kitchen with Mme. Carton, who was wearing her familiar pink satin bathrobe. Darcy felt like she was leaving home, and for a minute she wanted to stay, but she had to go back to her real life now, with her daughters, and face the divorce she never thought she'd have to go through.

When the car came, the driver took her bags. She had squared her accounts with Sybille the night before, and she had the thick folder of recipes she had carefully written down.

"Come back to see me," Sybille whispered to her as she hugged her, and there were tears in her eyes.

"I promise," Darcy answered, with a lump in her throat. "In the fall."

Mme. Carton patted Darcy's cheek like a doting grandmother, and without saying a word, Bill took her in his arms and held her tight, as she held him, knowing that it would never be the same for them again. The door to the future was wide open now, but it would close again when he got his new assignment and went back to his lonely life working for the government and defending freedom around the world.

"Take care of yourself," Darcy whispered to him.

"You too," was all he was able to say as he let her slip out of his arms, to go back to what was left of her old life.

Bill and Mme. Carton stood on the sidewalk as the car drove away and Darcy waved. What she had learned with all they'd been through together was that this day and this time would never come again. They had shared something very special, both terrifying and beautiful, and they had to let go of it now.

The car turned the corner and disappeared, as they headed to Zoe's apartment. She was waiting on the sidewalk with three duffel bags. There was a devastated look in her eyes, and her mother knew

what it was. She had said goodbye to the apartment where she had lived with Jean-Paul. She would remember it forever, and him.

It was a day of goodbyes. Darcy put her arms around her daughter and held her tight on the way to the airport as Zoe cried, and she fought back tears thinking of Bill. He had been important for a brief time in her life, and it was all they were meant to have. She knew she would remember him and this time forever.

Bill was sitting at the kitchen table with Mme. Carton by then, having another cup of coffee before he left for work.

"You will see her again, and so will I," she said, as much to cheer him up as herself. "She is a very rare woman, and you are a good man. Don't let her get away. Life is fleeting, fragile and unpredictable. We all just learned that lesson again. Now you must be brave," she said, and he smiled at her. "You lost one woman you loved, and it wasn't your fault. Don't lose another one." He nodded, wishing that life were different and he had met Darcy years ago. Now it was too late. He had chosen a different kind of life. He got up, put his cup in the sink, and looked out the window at the garden in full bloom, and then he turned and kissed Mme. Carton's cheek.

"Thank you. That's good advice. I wish I were younger. We make choices in life and have to honor them."

"You already have. You've been a spy for long enough, now have some fun," she said, and he laughed and hurried down the stairs to go to work. And for a moment he was sorry that he wasn't a spy, but he was just a man with a job to do that would take him halfway around the world to some desolate, dangerous place.

\* \* \*

The flight to New York took off on time. It felt strange to be in an airplane after they had been grounded for months. Darcy felt a faint ripple of fear, as others did too. What if the virus wasn't gone, if it was lingering somewhere, if it started again? She pushed the thoughts from her mind, took a few breaths, and tried to relax. She watched a movie, and had lunch, while Zoe slept. She'd been out late with her friends the night before, and it had been emotional for her leaving the apartment.

Darcy thought of Bill on the flight home. He had been a rock to hang onto in the storm, and a good man to have around. They would be friends now when they met again. Their time together had come and gone. She was sad about it, but they all had to look forward now, to the world that had been returned to them, like a gift.

They went through Customs in New York without a problem, as the officer welcomed them back to the United States. Zoe was beaming as they walked through the airport, while a porter pushed their bags.

"I thought I'd never get back here again," she said to her mother, as Darcy looked around them in awe. The airport had never looked so good.

"Yeah, I thought that too." But they had made it. They had survived. They had come home.

They drove into the city, and Darcy unlocked the front door of their townhouse. The housekeeper had been there and the house looked immaculate, as Zoe let out a war whoop, and raced up the stairs to her room. She was standing there grinning when her mother came up the stairs a minute later.

"I can't wait till Penny comes home," Zoe said, touching things, sitting on the bed, and looking around, drinking it all in. It felt like a miracle to both of them to be back there. Darcy had dreamed this a hundred times while they were confined in Paris, the image of home, and now it was real. With the time difference, it was only noon in New York, and Darcy went to her own room and looked around, suddenly remembering that Charlie was never coming home to this house again. She was going to live here alone, if Charlie would agree to let her stay, or was willing to sell her his half of the house. She didn't want to move. The girls had grown up there. And he was going to start a new life with another woman and their baby. She felt like someone was choking her as she thought about it. She walked through the bedroom to his dressing room, and all his clothes were there. They would have to be packed and sent to him, probably in Italy where he would be living. Without his stores now, Charlie didn't have to live in the states. Darcy had finally come home to everything familiar and now it was all going to change.

Zoe came through the door as Darcy was coming out of his dressing room, and she saw the look on her mother's face. Darcy looked devastated.

"Are you okay, Mom?"

"Yeah, fine, just looking around. It feels good to be home." But Zoe could see that there was a cloud in her mother's eyes. She had seen the future in those few minutes standing among all of Charlie's clothes. Soon it would be empty, and so would her life, with her daughters away in college and her husband gone. But she had learned in Paris that she was a survivor, and she couldn't let this destroy her. There were new chapters ahead and she had to be brave enough to face them. Living through the pandemic in France, far from home, had taught her how strong she was.

She took a quick walk around the house, and everything looked the same. Nothing had changed. But she had. She knew that now. She had taken some hard hits. She was braver than she'd been when she left three months before. And different. They all were. Even Zoe and Penny, with what they'd been through. And Charlie had to face his own new life. There would be more changes in store for all of them, when he told the girls about Flavia and the baby.

Darcy had come home to build a new life, and she was strong enough to do it. As she thought about it, it felt good to be home. This was the rock, the foundation, their base, their home, and they'd figure out the rest as they went along.

They met in the kitchen a little while later and made lunch, and then she and Zoe dragged their bags upstairs and started unpacking. Zoe smiled at her then, and looked happy. "It feels good to be home, doesn't it, Mom?" Darcy smiled at her and nodded.

"Yes, baby, it does," and this time she meant it.

She put everything away, and had almost finished when Bill called. She was surprised to hear from him, and it felt odd to hear him as she stood in her bedroom in New York.

"I called to make sure you got home okay. How does it feel?" he asked, as she listened to his voice that was so familiar to her now.

"It felt weird at first. I felt so different after Paris, and now it feels okay. I guess I am different, and my life is about to be very different." But she was getting used to the idea. It was as though she had thought the past few months wouldn't have happened and would be erased once she got home. But they had happened. None of it would be erased. And nothing would be exactly the same again.

"I miss you," he said in a low, husky voice.

"I miss you too." It was true, she did. She missed him more than she missed Charlie. Charlie was history now.

"Sybille gave me hell for letting you get away. Should I have stopped you?" he said wistfully.

"You couldn't have," she said. "This is my life, it's where I live. I had to come back here and face it all. And you have your life."

"I know. I'll see you soon, Darcy. Take good care of yourself."

"I will. You too, and thank you for calling." They hung up a minute later, and he was sorry he hadn't kissed her when he could have. He wondered if Sybille was right about life being fragile and unpredictable, or if it really was too late. He sat thinking about it and how empty the house seemed without her.

Darcy was smiling as she put the last of her sweaters away. It was nice of him to call her.

When Penny came home the next day, it was a scene of total jubilation. The girls hadn't seen each other in five months. They had all been through hell. And they were finally home, together and safe.

They had dinner in the kitchen and the twins couldn't tear themselves away from each other. They talked incessantly and were in and out of their mother's room a dozen times, as though they needed to be sure she was there.

At dinner, Zoe said she had called her father in Rome, and he was coming home in two weeks. Darcy didn't comment, which Penny noticed immediately, and the two girls talked about it in their room alone that night.

"Mom looks like someone died every time someone mentions Dad," Penny said to Zoe. "That's not a good sign."

"I know. I think something bad's going to happen when he gets home," Zoe said.

"I think something bad already happened," Penny added, "and Mom doesn't want to tell us." Zoe didn't disagree. She had thought that for two months, after their mother arrived in Paris from Rome.

"He must have done something really awful for her to look like that, and he said there were 'problems.'"

"We'll see when he gets here," Penny said quietly, but in the meantime, they had all survived their ordeals and they were home.

The twins slept in the same bed that night and clung to each other. Whatever had happened, or would happen, whatever they'd been through, they had survived it, and were together again. That was all that mattered.

# Chapter 14

In Italy, the Tedescos were still mourning Umberto. They had collected his ashes and had a small service with a priest and the entire family. They all agreed that life wasn't the same without him. Particularly for Francesca, who felt lost without his guiding hand and strong direction. Roberto and Stella felt it too, trying to run all the branches of the company. Roberto was in charge, but he consulted Stella a dozen times a day. More than ever before, she had a voice in the company, while Roberto took the credit, just as their father had. Stella realized that this was their chance to modernize and change slightly, but not so much that people would notice and resist. She tried to get Bianca on board with it, but pregnant, with three children, a demanding husband, and a big job designing all their sportswear and clothing lines, she was overwhelmed. Stella had a better vision for the directions she thought they should go in, and she worked closely with Roberto to make that happen. She didn't mind his getting all the credit, as long as the company reaped the benefits, and she thought it would.

Charlie had a lot to deal with, with all four of his stores going bankrupt. It was going to be a huge change in his life, and he and Roberto talked a lot about it. Roberto was impressed by how Charlie steered his ship with a positive thrust. Roberto was determined to set up a separate new business to deliver high-end luxury fashion goods online. It was a proven moneymaker for everyone who tried it in recent years, and those companies had survived two pandemics. The older brick-and-mortar model of department store hadn't, which told Charlie what he needed to know. Online selling was something Roberto had wanted to do for years too, and his father had strongly opposed it and stopped it from happening. Now they had the chance, if they combined their resources and raised some additional money to launch it, and Stella agreed. Bianca said she'd cast her vote with her sister. What they had to do was raise the money, and now felt like the right time. Not everyone had lost a fortune in this latest pandemic. It had toppled Charlie's empire, but others had withstood it, and had even made a healthy profit, if their overhead was low, or they had transformed their factories to produce other goods at the government's request. The pandemic had also taught governments in different countries to join forces and harness their resources jointly. Charlie also loved the idea of starting an online business with the Tedescos, because it would allow him to set up a strong base in Italy, and work from there.

Flavia was watching what he was doing closely. Her sales had suffered like everyone else's but only for a brief time. Her customers were back as soon as the confinement was over, hungry for new clothes and wanting to make up for lost time. She had a different customer from Tedesco, who served people who wanted to buy classics and basics that would last forever. They had a huge client base all over the world. Flavia's designs were more distinctive, and her clients would not want to wear them forever. They were looking for new and fresh and exciting, no matter how expensive. Flavia had a younger, bolder client than the more traditional family brands, and stores could barely keep her clothes in stock, with total disregard of the price tag. Every time she raised her prices, her customers followed. Charlie had helped her achieve that for the last three years. Within weeks, she was bouncing back from the pandemic and her sales figures demonstrated that, which was why both Stella and Roberto trusted his judgment. Charlie was a merchandising and marketing genius. He was excited about starting a new business in Italy, and a new life. He was starting over with a woman he loved and their child, and he liked the idea of living in Rome. He already did about half the time, and it was centrally located for travel in Europe, and both Rome and Milan were easy to get to from the States with the direct flights that were operational again. Everything was new in his life, and it made him feel young again. He even looked it.

With the confinement, Flavia's pregnancy seemed to have gone quickly. In May, she was six months pregnant and feeling well. And Charlie had regained his strength rapidly, with the good, healthy meals she provided and the love and attention she lavished on him. He was aware of it all the time. They were living a sane, wholesome life, and he wasn't on planes all the time and rushing to catch up, to be with her in Rome.

The one trip he was eager to make was to see his daughters in

New York. The confinement due to the virus had postponed it unduly, and he wanted to see his daughters as soon as possible. He had missed them terribly, and they were clamoring for his return. They knew nothing of what was happening, and Charlie didn't want it to get away from him completely before he had a chance to talk about the direction he was going in, professionally as well as personally. They had no idea that the bulk of his life and interests were sliding more and more onto the Rome side of the scale. He wanted them to know, and to visit him in Italy.

They would be on the move soon too, in a year when they graduated from college, and he wanted to welcome Penny into his new business, just as he would have when he had the stores. This would be a wonderful opportunity for her. He hoped that she would see it that way. She was worldly enough to understand the global implications, whereas Zoe was steeped in the art and culture of the eighteenth and nineteenth centuries. Business was not her strong suit or her interest. Charlie loved the model of the strong family business the Tedescos had, and he would welcome either or both of his daughters into his business at any time.

Charlie tried to get as much as possible in place and organized before he left for New York. Darcy had found a lawyer as soon as she got home and filed the divorce. The paperwork was sent to his attorney, and Charlie had to give them a list of his assets, which even he didn't know right now, entering bankruptcy proceedings for four stores. He didn't know yet what kind of money he had personally as part of his assets, but he intended to find out before he divided it up in a divorce. They didn't have a prenup. At the time they married, he thought he didn't need one, and he trusted Darcy even now. They were both civilized people and wanted to pay homage to their family and the good years they had spent as man and wife.

Flavia took him to the airport the morning he left for New York during the last week in May. He didn't know what to expect when he got there. He'd had no direct contact with Darcy, and he wasn't sure how angry she was, or what the girls had gleaned from their parents' cryptic comments. They knew that something had happened, but they weren't sure what. They were bright girls and had guessed that something was awry. They were waiting for him to come home and tell them.

Flavia was worried about their reactions to whatever Charlie would tell them, and that they would be furious with him and hate her. He recognized it as a possibility, but he intended to be honest with them. They had just turned twenty and were old enough to understand that parents had their own problems and that some marriages didn't survive. But it was more complicated than that with their parents, since he had lied to all of them for two years. He took full responsibility for it and wasn't going to deny it to them. He fully realized that they might never forgive him. It was part of the collateral damage of the situation he had created and not dealt with.

He kissed Flavia before he left her at the airport and reminded her to be careful. He still wanted her to wear a mask, just for good measure, and she said she didn't need it. There had been no new cases of the virus anywhere in Italy for a month, nor in France or several

European countries, and the borders were opening again. He had no problem returning to the United States, because he was a citizen, but the U.S. had been one of the last countries to reopen their borders, and only citizens and permanent residents could enter U.S. territory. He couldn't have brought Flavia with him even if he'd wanted to, which he didn't. The authorities were supposed to reopen the borders in the next two weeks, far quicker than in the previous pandemic where panic and less testing had kept the borders closed for months, before there was a vaccine for Covid-19.

He had made a reservation at a small hotel near the house, and didn't ask to stay at his home. The girls were not aware of that yet, and he didn't tell them, or they would have known immediately that the marriage was over. He had arranged for a moving company to pack his things and ship them to Italy. He had countless meetings, which were going to be painful, for the closure of his stores. An era had ended over a health crisis, which had changed the face of the world economy for now, and the U.S. was in better shape than many.

Penny and Zoe knew when he was arriving, and he had told them he would come straight home. They were desperate to see him and had promised to cook him dinner that night. Darcy had taught them how to make a few of her Paris recipes, and they wanted to do that for him, which he knew might not be possible or desirable after their meeting that afternoon. He was sure that Darcy wouldn't want him dining in her kitchen. He was nervous about seeing her.

He was tired and tense when he got out of the cab at his address. He stood looking at the building for a minute, and realized he didn't miss it. It was sad to admit, but in a way being confined in Italy had been a liberation for him, and he had had to make a choice of how and where he wanted to live when it was over. It would have been hard for Flavia to move to New York, with her booming business to run. It could be done, and people did it, with one foot in each country, but it was hard, particularly with a baby to deal with now, and a young child in a few years.

He wondered if she would want more children after this one. She was young enough to want several more, and in true Tedesco style, he suspected she would. He wasn't opposed to it, particularly in the close-knit family framework in which they lived. Having children constantly underfoot and part of every meal and event was part of being with Flavia, and there were always spare pairs of hands to help. Even Roberto walked around occasionally with one of Bianca's children in his arms, while engaged in animated conversation with someone else. It all seemed normal to them, and to Charlie it was a wonderful, warm, loving way to live. He had wanted more children with Darcy, but she always said she was too busy with the twins. The pregnancy had been too difficult, the birth too traumatic, and the first five or six years too frantic. She had no desire to do it again, but he didn't think the same was true of Flavia, unless something went very wrong at the birth, which he doubted would happen. She was healthy and young, and everything had gone smoothly so far, in spite of the virus in their midst. Charlie loved the warmth of her big Italian family. It wasn't how he and Darcy had grown up. Darcy was a product of the natural reserve of her own family, and preferred their style. The Tedescos' open Latin style would have made her uncomfortable. But Charlie loved it and how different it was from his own origins with his conservative Boston parents. He needed the warmth and affection the Tedescos offered, which Darcy could never give him, even though she loved him. She wasn't an exuberant, demonstrative person. Flavia met his needs better.

Charlie used his key to open the door and rang the bell at the same time. With a houseful of women, he wanted to give them fair warning. He shouted as he walked into the front hall and called out, "Man on the floor!" as men had done in all female dorms in college when he was young. Now those dorms didn't even exist, and the twins' generation didn't know about them. They all lived in co-ed dorms, which were unheard of then.

Zoe stuck her head out of her room first, gave a scream of glee, and rushed down the stairs to greet her father and threw her arms around him as he hugged her, just as glad to see her. Penny followed within seconds. He had his arms around both of them in the front hall as they laughed and talked, and Darcy appeared at the top of the stairs. She watched them for a few minutes and Charlie looked up at her. For a flash of an instant, it felt like old times, and then Darcy's smile faded, and he grew serious.

"Did you have a good trip?" she asked him from the top of the stairs. He nodded. He had noticed that his daughters looked more grown-up and even more beautiful than they had at the beginning of the year when he had last seen them. A lot had happened since then. The world had caved in, and they had been forced to mature beyond their years. The whole world had changed, and he had too. "Do you want something to eat?" Darcy offered, still from the distance, and he shook his head.

"I'm fine. I ate on the plane." She was pleased to see that he looked well, although he was thin. She guessed that he must have lost at least fifteen pounds, maybe more, from when he was sick. It was an

odd feeling, seeing him. He had been her husband for twenty years and now suddenly he wasn't. It was a hard shift to make, and a big transition. But she was finally getting used to it. She went back to her bedroom, and through it to her little sitting room. She wanted to leave Charlie alone with the girls. She didn't need or want to be there for the conversation they were about to have.

Charlie and the twins went into the living room because it was close at hand. The art was bright and cheery and some of the paintings were valuable. It reminded him that they would have to list their separate property and decide what to do about what they'd bought jointly, and he would have to decide if there was anything he wanted and would exclude from the property settlement. Darcy had to do the same. She'd been dragging her feet about doing it when she'd been back. It was so final it depressed her. She felt breathless every time she thought of the divorce. She had told her doctor, who told her it was from anxiety, and she had certainly had her share of that in the past few months.

The girls settled into two big cozy chairs and sank into them. They were white Italian mohair, and Zoe slung her legs in jeans and her feet in her favorite sneakers over the chairs. Charlie didn't comment. It wasn't his house now.

"I'm so glad to see you both, and you both look great, in spite of everything that happened," he said as openers. He felt as though he was about to jump off the high dive. He just hoped there was water in the pool, or would be when he landed.

"We're glad you're okay too, Dad. We were so worried about you when you were sick." He nodded. He had been worried too. Several times he was sure he was dying, and by some miracle, he hadn't.

"It was very scary." He took a breath. "Your mom and I have wanted to talk to you for a while. Some things have happened. Serious things. I made some very big mistakes, but everything happens for a reason. Your mom and I have talked about this a lot, and she's been amazing. I don't think I could be as gracious under fire as she's been," he said. The twins were silent, dreading what was coming. They thought they could guess, but let him say his piece, out of respect for him. "Sometimes things happen in a marriage. One or both people change. You're not the same person anymore, or you do something you shouldn't. Or you just run out of gas. It's important to do things in the right order in life, and I didn't. I think somewhere along the way, your mom and I ran out of gas. We got tired, and busy, too busy. I traveled a lot. She got wrapped up in her blog. I'll try to give you the short version. I want to be honest with you. I got involved with someone in Italy. I shouldn't have. I didn't deal with it. I didn't tell your mom. I bounced back and forth for two years, between the two of them."

"You *cheated* on Mom?" Zoe interrupted him with a look of outrage, and he nodded.

"Yes, I did. It all came out in February. It had to happen. It couldn't go on the way it was. To sum it up, I lied to your mother for two years. And she's right, our marriage could never recover from it. It takes trust to make a marriage work. I blew it. I did. We weren't attentive enough to our marriage. And I got involved with someone else. We're getting a divorce now." There was no way to dress it up and he didn't try. Telling them was the hardest thing he had ever done.

Both girls looked pained then, although they had half expected it.

And then he kicked the field goal through the goal posts, with the rest. "And I'm getting married when the divorce is final, to Flavia Tedesco. We've been together for two years. And for the record, she *never* asked me to get divorced, not once. We're having a baby in August, a little boy." He had emptied all of it onto the floor in front of them. There were no secrets left. Their jaws had literally dropped with his final revelations, and neither of them said a word. And then Zoe jumped to her feet and looked at him, her green eyes blazing.

"Well, now we know who you are, don't we. A liar and a cheat. And you're getting *married* and having a baby? Are you kidding, Dad? What do you expect us to do? Applaud? Carry the bouquet for this woman or attend the delivery and cut the cord? Are you crazy enough to think we're supposed to be happy for you? And I don't care if she's the Queen of England. What you did is disgusting. I can't believe Mom is letting you into the house to see us." She had said it from halfway across the room, and Charlie didn't complain, argue, or try to stop her. He knew he deserved it.

"I'm sorry, Zoe. You're right. It's not a good story. But Flavia is a decent woman. She got caught in my mess. She could be a good friend to you, if you let her."

"I have friends. I don't need her to be my friend, Dad, and she's not much of a human being if she cheated with you for two years." Charlie didn't bother to make her a speech about how complicated life was, and how love was unpredictable and caused people to do strange things. Penny stood up then, and looked at him sadly, as though he had broken her heart, as well as her mother's. Her eyes were full of sorrow, for all of them.

"I'm sorry, Dad," was all she said, and followed Zoe out of the room, up the stairs, and into their own room, where Zoe slammed the door with ear-shattering force. She sat on her bed, too angry to even cry as she stared at her sister.

"I can't believe it. He's a dick. I can't believe he did that to Mom. No wonder Mom looked like that when she showed up early from Rome. I wonder if she walked in on them in bed or something. She looked like someone had died the first time I saw her. That's when I called you. I told you it was something big. You didn't believe me."

"I believe you now." Penny looked crushed, for them and their mother. It was a total betrayal and had gone on for two years. It sounded like he had told them all of it, which was at least something, and he took full responsibility. But what he'd done was so much worse than some small gesture.

"And I can't believe they're having a baby," Zoe fumed, pacing around the room. "He's fifty-two years old. Why does he need a baby?"

"And it's a boy," Penny said. "He's going to forget about us in five minutes. I think we've just been fired." It felt like it to them. Out with the old, in with the new.

"I think that was his goodbye speech," Zoe said, and lay down on Penny's bed, next to where she was sitting. They were like puppies, always on top of each other. "And where's he going to live now? In New York or with her? What's going to happen to us? Will he and Mom sell the house?" He had told them none of the practicalities that pertained to them to reassure them. "I don't want to see him again," Zoe said suddenly. Penny looked miserable.

"He's still our father," Penny reminded her.

"He may be yours, but he doesn't have to be mine, if I say he isn't. He'll probably never visit us now anyway. And that explains why he went to Rome all the time."

"He has business there," Penny said. "A lot of it."

"Not anymore. He's closing the stores. They went bust during the pandemic," she reminded her.

"They probably would have anyway. It's an outdated model," Penny said. She knew more about it and took an interest.

"I guess all we need to know is that he screwed Mom over, they're getting divorced, he's getting married, and having a baby. That pretty much sums it up." Penny was crying as Zoe said it, and only Zoe's fury at her father kept her from throwing herself on her bed and sobbing. And they both felt terrible for their mother and had new respect for her.

Their father had made his way up the stairs by then and was sitting in Darcy's study talking to her. She could see from his face how the meeting with the twins had gone. He had just told her what had happened and what Zoe said. "I wanted to be straight with them. I didn't want to dress it up and make excuses."

"It's a lot for them to digest. Especially with Flavia and the baby. They'll come around. They love you no matter what you do. You need to give them time now, to get used to the idea. It's a shock for them."

"What if they never forgive me, and they never see me again?" She didn't want to say that he should have thought of that for the two years while he was having fun in Rome. The twins were humans too, adults now, not children, and had feelings of their own, and values and standards they held their parents to.

"They'll see you, and forgive you. It may take a while." He nod-ded. The girls had brought reality home to him. He had come to New York to face his daughters, tell them the truth, negotiate his divorce settlement, and file bankruptcy for the stores he had poured his life into for twenty-five years and had lost to the pandemic. It was a time for endings for him, not just beginnings. Now the endings had all piled up on him at once.

"Did you get the papers my lawyer sent you?" Darcy asked him. He nodded. He felt as though he had just lost his daughters and his heart was aching. Darcy knew the feeling well. It was hard to feel sorry for him, although she tried to be compassionate about it. But some bumps along the way were going to be inevitable. She knew how tough Zoe could be on both of them. She was right this time. Penny was more forgiving. "We should get the property settlement done while you're here," she reminded him. "My lawyer did my list of assets. He needs yours."

"I don't know what I'll have left after the stores go. Probably not much for a while. But whatever cash I've got, I'm going to give you half of it. And both houses, and everything in them, some cash and support for you and the girls." That had been his plan all along. He was coming to Flavia with very little in his pockets. It was the way he wanted it, and she agreed. Flavia was doing well with her line and was about to get her share of the inheritance from her father, which was sizable. Tedesco had been a huge moneymaker for a long time, even after the first pandemic. It embarrassed Charlie to bring so little to the table at his age, but he felt he owed it to Darcy, and Flavia wanted to let him do what he felt was right. He was a generous man, when he could be. And he'd been married to Darcy for a long time and had children with her.

"You don't need to do all that for me, Charlie. Don't strip yourself out of guilt. We can sell the Southampton house if you need cash."

"You and the girls love it. What I did was wrong. I can at least leave you comfortable after twenty years of marriage." She would rather have had their marriage than two houses and half his money, but that wasn't an option. And she didn't want him back now. It really was over. She knew it when she saw him. He wasn't hers anymore, and she didn't want him. She had already healed more than she'd realized, after her discoveries in Rome. She was numb to him now. "Let's let the lawyers figure it out," Charlie said.

"How long are you here for?" she asked him.

"As long as it takes to get everything settled. Maybe a month, or longer."

"Let's try to finish it by then. I don't want to be haggling over the pots and pans and the vacuum cleaner for the next six months."

"Neither do I," he said with a sigh.

"Where are you staying?" He named a hotel nearby. "I'll tell the girls."

"I doubt I'll hear from them," he said somberly and stood up. "It was to be expected. I couldn't do anything else except level with them." Darcy nodded. He was right, and he should have leveled with her too. She wasn't angry at him anymore. Somehow the terror of the pandemic and being confined in France had healed that. She just wanted to move forward now. She didn't want to cry over the past. He was just starting to pay penance for what he'd done. She had no idea how the girls would react and where they'd land in the end. Maybe Penny would forgive him and Zoe wouldn't, or not for a long time. But she thought they'd both come around in the end, and she said that to Charlie. He hoped she was right.

He called Flavia when he got to the hotel. He sighed when she answered, and she could guess how it had gone. She had expected it to be hard. Charlie had been more optimistic, as long as he was honest with them. The twins had been harsher than he expected, and Zoe needed her pound of flesh to make him pay for his sins.

"How did it go?" Flavia asked him.

"It was awful. Zoe mostly, but Penny looked heartbroken." He told her about it, and she wasn't surprised. "Darcy thinks they'll come around. I'm not so sure. Not Zoe anyway. Or not for a very long time."

"We don't have to get married, you know, if you want to wait." She was quiet and reasonable, as always, and kind.

"I don't want to wait. I want to marry you yesterday. Because of the pandemic and the confinement, the divorce won't be final now until November or December, at the earliest. I wanted to get married before the baby, and we can't even do that. We're a family, I want us to be married."

"I don't have to be, I was willing to have the baby without being married originally. We can even wait a year or two if the girls need the time to come around."

"They will or they won't," Charlie said clearly. "We're getting mar-

ried as soon as the ink is dry on my divorce." She smiled when he said it.

"Fine. Then we know where that stands. Just give them time, Charlie. Let them get used to the idea. You hit them with a lot today. The divorce, me, and the baby."

"I will. It's just hard hearing things like that from your kids. But I deserve it."

"We both do. They may wind up hating me too. I was part of that lie, and now I'm adding a baby to their life. Were they upset about that? They must have been."

"I think so. It was the whole package. All of it."

He dealt with the stores next, which was complicated and would take some time. And simultaneously, he and his lawyer drafted a divorce settlement, and submitted it to Darcy's lawyer. His own lawyer was unhappy with it.

"Are you sure you want to give her all that?"

"It's for my kids in the end, and Darcy deserves it," Charlie responded.

She was ending up with the fruits of his labors for all the years they'd been married. It seemed right to him. She had been a good wife, and he felt as though he owed her a lot because of how it had ended.

He had a team of lawyers working on the bankruptcy, and in the end, they did it well. He was able to salvage a very reasonable amount of money, and he split it with Darcy. She kept both houses.

What he had left was enough to start the business with Roberto. He wouldn't have much more than that. But that was enough, and if their online business was as profitable as he thought, he would have plenty of money two or three years from now. He'd done it before and he'd do it again. He felt that he had been honorable with Darcy. She was embarrassed by his generosity, but she stopped arguing with him about it. She would leave the houses to the girls one day, one for each.

And as Darcy had predicted, Penny saw him for lunch before he left. She was still upset for her mother, but at least they connected and he could talk to her. Zoe wouldn't see him, or even respond to his texts. He wasn't surprised. And all he wanted at the end of four very tough weeks was to get back to Flavia in Rome. It had been a long month, it was a long flight, and he slept all the way back to Rome. His heart ached whenever he thought of his daughters. And he had done his best materially for Darcy. She was well set, but it didn't change what he'd done, and he knew it. His only reward was Flavia and his son. And he thought they were worth it.

# Chapter 15

Bill Thompson kissed Sybille Carton's smooth powdered cheek on a sunny morning in June when he finally left Paris. He'd been there for four months, and Darcy had left a month before. He had called her a few times since she left. He missed talking to her every day. She said that all the preliminary work on the divorce was done, and her ex-husband had just gone back to Rome. She said he'd been generous with her. In Bill's eyes, that didn't make up for what he'd done. But Darcy was satisfied for her children's sake and seemed at peace about the end of the marriage. She told him that Zoe hadn't seen her father again before he left. She said she never would again, but Darcy thought she'd relent. She had a punishing nature, and wasn't ready to forgive her father for what he had done to her mother, no matter what Darcy said. Bill agreed, and thought it was unforgivable. Darcy didn't deserve that, no matter how busy she'd been with her blog.

Mme. Carton looked at Bill long and hard as she stood in front of the house with him, waiting for a car from the U.S. Embassy to pick him up. She still wasn't too clear on what his job was, and she called him a spy because it was simpler and always made him laugh.

"Are you going to see Darcy?" she asked him sternly.

"I am."

"Don't lose her," she admonished him. "You need each other. We don't get many chances in life. You couldn't win the first one," with his wife terminally ill. "If you lose this one, you'll have only yourself to blame for it, and you'll always regret it. Don't be a coward. And you can't be a spy forever." He smiled. She was right about that, al-though he was a high-level advisor, not a spy. His job kept him soli-tary, and he had seen another path with Darcy. He just wasn't sure if he had the courage to follow it, or if that path was meant for him, or someone else. He was well suited to his job. But another round of harsh living in military conditions, with a high risk factor on a daily basis—it was well paid, but he was no longer sure it was worth it. Darcy had sparked a doubt in his mind, and so had Sybille Carton. He had spent some of the happiest months of his life in Paris, even during the confinement.

The car came, he kissed Sybille again and saluted her as they drove away. He was traveling in a plain gray suit, a blue shirt, and a navy tie, and looked like any other businessman flying from Paris to Washington, D.C. He had briefings at the Pentagon for the next four weeks for his new job, and had to report to CIA headquarters in Vir-ginia. He had made a dinner date with Darcy in two weeks. He was going to New York for the night on his first day off between briefings.

She'd been friendly and funny when they talked, and he had con-firmed the date by text when he got his schedule. The post wasn't too bad this time. It wasn't as rugged as the last one. A year in South Korea, with plenty of intrigue to keep him busy. It sounded interesting, with a good supervising agent he'd worked with before and liked.

Bill sent Darcy a text when he arrived, but after that he was in meetings and briefings constantly, many of them about the time he'd spent in Paris and the meetings he attended there, and the reams of information that had been shared with him, much of it contradictory. But everyone agreed in every country now that the pandemic was over. There hadn't been a single new case anywhere in two months. It was good news for the world.

The morning of his dinner date with Darcy, he took the train to New York. He was excited about seeing her. He arrived in Penn Station and took a cab to the hotel where he was staying in Midtown. For some reason, it was popular with CIA agents. There was a well-concealed office a few blocks away, and it was convenient and not too expensive, and it would be a short cab ride to Darcy's house. As he rode to the hotel, he marveled at how small freedoms they had been deprived of for two months had become guilty pleasures. A ride in a car, a trip on the train, a walk in a park, being able to stroll down the street. Social distancing had been relaxed and you could go to a restaurant without wearing a mask or feeling panicked that the person next to you could infect you. And a night out like the one he'd planned with Darcy felt like a vacation. The whole world was coming back to life, like the petals of a flower unfurling in the summer sun after a hard winter.

She had told him she was moving to the Hamptons soon for two months. He was scheduled to leave for South Korea in mid-July but had told her he would try to visit her once in the Hamptons before he left.

He checked into the hotel and sent her a text. Sybille Carton's warnings came to mind, and he smiled. He showered and changed before he left the hotel for dinner. He had made a reservation at a small French restaurant near her house that she'd told him about in Paris. She'd written about it in her blog as one of the things she missed. She made it sound so appealing that he wanted to go there with her.

He had continued following her blog after she left and had seen that she'd been busy since she'd gotten to New York a month before. He always enjoyed her blog and could see why it was such a big success. She had just over a million followers now after the confinement.

It was such a pretty, balmy evening that Bill walked from his hotel to her house. He hadn't been to New York in a few years, and enjoyed the bustle of activity, the cabs speeding by, the people walking their dogs. When he got to Central Park, he walked alongside it, enjoying the trees and the flowers and the young couples holding hands. It was a beautiful spring night.

When he got to her house, he rang the doorbell, and a pretty, dark-haired young woman opened it. She was the image of Darcy and he guessed that she was her other daughter. He had met Zoe briefly in Paris and remembered that she was an equally pretty petite blonde. The two girls were as different as Darcy had said. He felt like a very young man coming to pick up his date, and smiled when he introduced himself to Penny as she held the door open wide. She was wearing pink denim shorts and a T-shirt and sandals, and he could easily imagine that she looked exactly like her mother at the same age.

"She's upstairs, I'll get her," she said, and led him into the living room to sit down. He liked the art on the walls and the house felt open and airy and friendly, and there was a big picture window at the back of the house that looked out on a deck and a garden. The house had a nice feeling to it. It was warm and welcoming. He was admiring the garden when Darcy came down the stairs in a white silk dress with a matching jacket and high heels. He was so used to seeing her in her lockdown outfits that she stunned him for a minute. She was beautiful, with her long hair in a sleek ponytail and her nails manicured, with small diamond studs on her ears and her makeup perfectly done. He had only seen her wear makeup a few times.

"Wow!" he said as she walked toward him, and he smiled. "You look fantastic!" He looked handsome too in a dark blue summer suit, with impeccably shined shoes, a white shirt, and a pale blue Hermès tie he'd bought in Paris before he left.

"You look pretty good too, for a spy," she said, and he laughed. He saw her two daughters scamper down the stairs and head toward the kitchen, and she called them into the living room to meet him, and introduced them. They were exact opposites in every way, one tall and one petite, one dark and one fair, Penny smiling shyly, and Zoe studying him intently, ready to pass judgment on him. Darcy had explained that he had been the other tenant in the elegant Airbnb where she had spent the confinement. The girls chatted with him for a few minutes, and then left to go to the kitchen.

"They're beautiful, both of them, and so totally different. No one would ever guess they're twins."

"Different personalities too," Darcy said, as she offered him a drink and he said he'd wait till the restaurant. He couldn't take his eyes off her when they sat down in the living room. She looked as he had remembered her, but even better in her New York life, where she attended events, and influenced people, and informed them of what was going on in the world and what she thought about it. She was a very striking, beautiful woman. He'd been aware of it in Paris, but they were all so anxious and tense that no one cared about being chic or wearing makeup or high heels. He felt mildly intimidated by how impressive she was. "How's Washington?" she asked him.

"Interesting. Always. There's a lot going on at the moment, and a lot of debriefings about the pandemic. They claim we won't have another one in this century. I'm not sure how they know that, but it sounds good to me."

"Me too," she said with relief. They left a few minutes later for the restaurant, after saying good night to the girls. He didn't ask her about Charlie or the divorce, or the girls' reaction to him. He didn't want to bring up a painful subject. They strolled down Madison Avenue, past all the shops, and got to the French restaurant tucked into a side street a few minutes later. They were given a table in the garden. It looked very French, and reminded them both of Sybille Carton.

"I miss her," he said with a smile. "She was like the mother I never had." She knew his own mother had died young and his father had been a harsh taskmaster, a "Navy man." After his mother's death, Bill had grown up with no maternal or female attention, and had learned to be without it, until his wife. But he only had her for a few years, and then he lost her. He had been solitary without deep attachments for a long time.

"I'm working on something for her," Darcy said of Sybille. "It's a surprise. I hope I can get back there in the fall. I always go at the end of September for fashion week." Thanks to him, the memories she had of their confinement had a nostalgic quality now.

They ordered dinner, and he told her about some of the meetings he'd attended in Washington that he was allowed to speak of, and she finally asked him about his next assignment over dessert. He hesitated before he answered.

"Well," he said, "I have an interesting choice. Something of a dilemma. I think the pandemic changed me. Or Sybille did. Or you did. I've been assigned to an area in South Korea that needs help. Fairly rugged physical conditions as always, a superior I've worked with before and like. No expected violence, although that's always a possibility. A one-year assignment, and possibly something in the Middle East after that, in oil country. Or, if I listen to our friend in Paris, I can take the leap and start my own consulting business now. I'm considering high-level security with an industrial espionage feature, which I'm good at, and which would make me a spy according to Sybille. I was saving that for my future, but I'm turning fifty, and I'm not sure I want to face a Korean winter, living in a barracks, and waiting a year until I see you again. It's up in the air at the moment, while I think about it. One option is everything I'm familiar with and know I can do well, the other is an unknown, about whether I can get my own private agency off the ground and make a success of it. I could take a leave of absence for a year and give it a try, an agency of my own, and see how it goes. I can start my own consulting business now, and not wait another five or ten years to do it, or I can stay on the path I'm on, go to Korea, and do what I know. And not look back." She looked intrigued as she listened, and he searched her eyes for the answer. "What do you think, Darcy?" She paused for a few seconds and smiled as she answered.

"Do you really want to know?" she asked him, and he nodded. "I think the leap of faith now. Sybille isn't wrong. Life is fleeting. We don't know what will happen tomorrow. The pandemic taught us that. If you have a dream, grab it. You know you can do it. And spending another year in a barracks doesn't sound too appealing to me. Where would you set up the agency?"

"I can set it up anywhere, and I'd be traveling all over the world on private assignments if the business takes off. I'd want to steal a few really good operatives from my current employer, so I don't have to do all the missions myself. I have to admit, it sounds exciting. A lot more so than South Korea, and the Middle East a year later. I've done all that. Maybe it's time for something new." As he said it, he moved his hand slightly across the table and held hers, as they looked into each other's eyes and found Paris all over again. But they were free to enjoy it this time. They had laid the foundation in Paris, and had never taken advantage of it, but with a new career and a new life, the possibilities were infinite. "Sybille told me to stop running. I've thought about it a lot, and I think she may be right," he said.

"I think she'd be proud of you," Darcy said softly, "and I would be too."

"That's the direction I'm leaning. Maybe twenty years working for the government is enough."

She nodded. "You can't be a spy forever," she said, and the waiter looked at them as he set their dessert down in front of them, and Bill laughed.

"You are an amazing woman, Darcy Gray. You've changed my life, and made me ask myself some serious questions about my future."

"No, *you've* changed your life, and opened the door, and that's when exciting things happen."

"If I do this, can I come to Paris with you when you go back?"

She smiled at him, and they were still holding hands. "I think that's a very good idea. We can stay with Sybille."

"Of course." He was smiling, thinking of the extraordinary times waiting for them. He had already known what he wanted to do. But he wanted her blessing. "I think it would be only half the cost this time," he said.

"How do you figure that?" she asked, amused. "Is she lowering her prices?"

"It seems to me, if we're exploring new territory on our big adventure, that we'd only need one room instead of two this time. What do you think?" he asked her, holding his breath for her answer.

"I think it's a very good idea." She smiled at him. Everything was changing in his life. Or it might, if he had the courage to do it. She made him brave, and happy.

They walked back to her house after dinner. He had liked the restaurant as much as she did. He was excited about the agency he wanted to start. He had needed a sign from her. It meant retiring from the CIA, but at nearly fifty, he felt ready to do that. He had wanted to see her again before he handed in his resignation. Sybille Carton's words hadn't fallen on deaf ears. He couldn't run away from love forever. Living in tents and dodging snipers was easy for him, it was familiar. Love wasn't. He might lose Darcy one day. She might leave him, or die, or something terrible could happen. But something wonderful could too. And from what he could tell, it just had.

They stopped outside her house when they got there, and he pulled her close to him. He kissed her, which was long overdue. But they knew each other well now, and had lived through a crisis together. He knew who she was and what he was getting, and so did she. There were no bad surprises lurking. He would never betray her, and she wasn't going anywhere.

"I'm sorry I waited so long," he whispered.

"You were worth waiting for. I've never been in love with a spy before," she whispered back. And he laughed and kissed her again.

Bill handed in his resignation two weeks later, and spent most of July in Washington getting organized and interviewing agents he wanted to hire, and found three good ones he knew well who were willing to leave the CIA and wanted to work for him. One was based in Washington, and two in New York. It didn't matter where they lived.

He came to the Hamptons to spend a weekend with Darcy and the twins. The girls liked him, and the four of them had fun together. It was a part of life he'd never known. Life in a family with two girls.

He belonged to the CIA until the end of August, and then he was free. He was planning to launch his agency in September, and the girls were enormously impressed that he worked for the CIA.

"Is he a spy, Mom?" Zoe asked her with an intense expression, and her mother laughed.

"I honestly don't know. Maybe so." But whether he was or not, she knew that Mme. Carton would be pleased with the way things were working out. And so was she. They were headed in the right direction at just the right speed for both of them.

# Chapter 16

Philippe and Mariette Nattier did something they hadn't done in thirty years. Their factories had been returned to their original purposes, hers producing perfume, and his manufacturing hair dryers, vacuum cleaners, space heaters, and all his very efficient inventions. And when their factories were closed for the month of August, Philippe organized it without telling her, and booked them into the Hotel du Cap in Cap d'Antibes for a month, with a private cabana where they could spend the days alone, lying in the sun, having lunch, swimming in the sea or the pool. They dressed elegantly for dinner, and went to their favorite restaurants in the area, the Colombe d'Or in Saint-Paul de Vence being one of them. The owner was pleasantly surprised to welcome them back and still remembered them from years before long ago.

They took walks, and went to Monte Carlo for dinner and dancing and a stop at the casino. They had both forgotten how much they loved their vacations in the South of France. It was a second honeymoon, and so much better than the first one. They were making up for lost time, and the three decades they had wasted being angry at each other. The confinement had given them beauty for ashes. They couldn't remember why they were always so unhappy before. The bitterness they had fostered for so many years had vanished when Mariette got sick, and then survived, and Philippe realized how much he loved her.

When the rest of the Tedesco family went to their house in Sardinia in August, Charlie and Flavia stayed in Rome. The baby's due date was only two weeks away. The tourists were in town, people were traveling again, but most of the wealthy locals had left for their summer homes in Capri, Sardinia, Puglia, or Corsica, and Flavia always loved the city in summer when it was a little less crowded. She was busy putting the finishing touches on the nursery. Charlie had been busy for two months, setting up his new online business with Roberto. They were a perfect combination, with Roberto's expertise as a manufacturer of luxury clothing, and Charlie's extensive retail experience. They asked Stella, Bianca, and Flavia's design advice frequently. It was fun working on it together.

Bianca was seven months pregnant and said she felt like a whale when they left for the house they had rented in Capri. Paolo wanted a break from the family. And Flavia was perfectly happy to stay in the city. They went out for dinner every night, to little trattorias, many of them in Trastevere, across the Tiber.

She had finished her collection for Milan Fashion Week in September early, so she could take time off with the baby, and she planned to be back on her feet in time to do model fittings in late September. Her pregnancy had been easy, and Charlie loved being with her all the time, while they waited for their son to appear. He was due on the tenth of August, and there was no sign of him yet when she saw her doctor the day before. She was huge, but Charlie thought she looked beautiful with her golden curls and her enormous belly. Every other part of her was thin, but the baby was enormous.

Stella called her every day from Porto Cervo in Sardinia, to see if there was any sign of the baby yet, but there wasn't so far. They went to her mother's house on some days, so Flavia could use the pool. Francesca was visiting friends in Tuscany, as she did every year. And Nonna Graziella stayed in Florence, and was doing well. She had managed to escape the virus completely by staying home and not having any visitors.

Charlie and Flavia had just come home from a relaxed dinner at their favorite trattoria on her due date. It started so gently that she was sure it wasn't labor. She had pains every twenty minutes or so, and she and Charlie lay on their bed and watched movies, waiting to see if the pains would stop or continue. Two hours later, nothing had changed, and she was sure it was false labor, but then the pains took a leap to ten minutes and got more serious. It was midnight by then, and she didn't want to go to the hospital yet. It still seemed too early to her. She was relaxed about it. Her sisters had warned her that it would be agony, and this didn't seem strong enough to take seriously, so they stayed home and she fell asleep, as Charlie smiled and watched her. He could hardly wait to see their baby.

He had just fallen asleep himself when he heard a cry next to him and turned to see Flavia reaching for him. She clutched his arm and couldn't speak until the pain was over.

"Oh my God, Charlie, the baby is coming." She had another pain and he leapt out of bed and put his pants and shoes on, and buttoned his shirt, while she reached for him again. He knew instantly that they had waited too long. Her sisters had misled her. "It's coming," she said between contractions. They were five minutes apart.

"It is not coming," Charlie said in a firm voice. "I am not delivering this baby." He called the doctor on his cellphone, who told them to get to the hospital immediately. It was only fifteen minutes away. "We have to go. The doctor says to get you there now."

"I don't want to. I can't move," she said, and started to cry. He picked her up and carried her to the car as quickly as he could. He didn't want to hurt her. The pains were almost constant as he started his car and took off, Flavia clutching his arm again. It felt like something out of a movie. It was one-thirty in the morning, and traffic was still heavy. He darted in and out of the Roman traffic madness, almost hit a couple on a Vespa but managed to dodge them, and raced into the hospital parking lot. He stopped the car and rushed into the emergency entrance to get someone to help them. A nurse came with him at a dead run, two orderlies with a gurney right behind them. Flavia was gasping for breath and crying as the orderlies lifted her out of the car and onto the gurney and ran her into the hospital, with Charlie running next to her, holding her hand.

"Charlie, this is awful," she said, sobbing. "It's worse than my sisters told me." And a lot faster. He had never been so frightened in his life. He thought he'd have to deliver the baby himself in the car on the street.

They wheeled her into an exam room, and left her on the gurney, as she clutched Charlie's arm, and two more nurses came into the room and said her doctor had been called, and the obstetrician on duty was coming. She screamed when one of the nurses examined her, and the nurse smiled as soon as she had. "I can see the baby's head, just push gently." Charlie felt faint as he watched the scene in front of him and realized how close he had come to delivering their baby. Flavia was screaming and the nurses were telling her to push. Two of them held her legs, Charlie held her shoulders, and an instant later, there was a wail in the room, and a strong cry, and Flavia had stopped screaming and was smiling, as the nurse cut the cord and then lifted the baby gently, wrapped him in a blanket, and laid him in her arms. Charlie stood beside her and cried, and bent down to kiss her.

"You have a beautiful big son," the nurse who had delivered him said proudly, as the obstetrician on duty walked into the room and smiled at the happy scene. They took the baby from Flavia then to weigh him and clean him, while the doctor checked her. The placenta was delivered, and five minutes later the baby was back in her arms.

"He weighs nine pounds," one of the nurses told them. "That was the fastest delivery I've ever seen. Next time you'd better leave your house a little earlier, or your husband will be delivering the baby." They all laughed, and Charlie looked at Flavia adoringly, as she held their son.

"That wasn't so bad," she said, shaking, but she was smiling. "It was easy. Stella said I'd have to push for three or four hours, especially with a first baby." It was more like three or four minutes. She had completely missed all the signs of early labor.

They cleaned her up while Charlie held their son and looked at him in amazement. He really was a miracle. He looked more like a several-months-old baby than a newborn, and was a big, healthy boy. Charlie had been worried for weeks that Flavia would have to have a C-section because the baby was so big, but he had slid right out of her with two pushes. When they settled her into a bed in a private room, she looked like nothing had happened. And she had never looked more beautiful to Charlie.

"Can we call him Umberto, after my father?" Flavia asked him, with tears in her eyes. They had thought that it was bad luck to name him before he arrived, and Charlie smiled.

"Of course." Charlie called Stella, Bianca, and Roberto, although it was two-thirty in the morning, but they were delighted with the news and said they'd call everyone else, and he sent a text to the twins that their brother had been born. It was still early in New York, and Penny sent back a text congratulating them, and Zoe didn't respond, which didn't surprise her father, but hurt anyway.

Charlie and Flavia lay on the bed in her room and looked at little Umberto in wonder, sound asleep in a little plastic bassinette, and they finally fell asleep themselves at six in the morning and woke up when the nurse came to check Flavia at nine. At nine-thirty, everyone started calling and the phone rang all day. And armloads of flowers arrived.

Flavia took a shower, did her hair, and put on lipstick, and looked like a movie star to Charlie as he gazed at her. He was surprised and embarrassed when he got a text from Darcy that said only "Congratulations." It brought back memories for both of them of another time, when the twins were born, so tiny in their incubators and so fragile. Umberto looked like a sturdy little guy, and he was ravenous when a nurse put him to the breast, even though Flavia didn't have milk yet. Everything had been so simple and so natural and so easy, as though it was meant to be that way, and he wondered how many more babies they would have as he looked at her. He had a feeling this was just the beginning. The beginning of a long happy life with her and many children.

At five o'clock, the door to Flavia's room burst open, and Roberto and Stella and Massimo walked in. They had flown up from Sardinia with an aunt that Charlie had only met once, two cousins he had never seen, and Stella's oldest son. Everyone admired the baby, and Roberto and Stella held him. The noise in the room sounded like a cocktail party, and Roberto poured the champagne he had brought. Charlie grinned, looking at the scene as Flavia lay there, holding their son, with her family around her. They were the classic big Italian family. Francesca called them from Tuscany, and Nonna Graziella from Florence. Flavia was exhausted by the time the visitors left. They flew back to Sardinia, and the room was finally quiet, as Charlie held their son and Flavia fell asleep.

In the morning, they went home with their baby boy. There were visitors in and out of the house all week, bringing gifts and food and flowers and balloons, wanting to see the baby, congratulating both of them. It wasn't what Charlie was used to, but he loved it. They were surrounded by a world full of love. And Flavia was managing very well. Umberto nursed easily, and he slept in his mother's arms between feedings except when Charlie was holding him, or some visiting relative.

Charlie called Zoe the day after Umberto was born and apologized to her again for his failures as a husband and a father. It was heartfelt, and this time she relented. He asked her if she and Penny would come over for a few days before they went back to school. He wanted them to meet their baby brother, and Flavia, and to be part of the lovefest around them. He had handled the affair badly and betrayed Darcy, but the end result was a union that was solid and based on the right values, and he wanted the twins to be part of his and Flavia's life too.

Penny talked Zoe into it, even Darcy encouraged her to go, and make peace with her father. Zoe finally agreed. They came for the Labor Day weekend before they started school and flew from Rome to Boston after three days of people hugging and kissing them and welcoming them. It was a constant feast of people and joy. The twins looked startled by all of it, and their father thanked them for coming. It had meant a lot to him, and Flavia made as big a fuss over them as everyone else did over the baby. She didn't say it to them, but she had two daughters now too.

Penny turned to Zoe on the plane to Boston. "You have to admit, she's nice. Dad looks happy. And the baby is kind of cute."

"He was a shit to Mom," Zoe said, glaring at her twin, and then she relaxed. "But yes, Flavia is nice. And I guess they're happy."

"Can we go to the wedding?" Penny asked her. Everyone had

asked her about it while they were there. Flavia and Charlie were planning to get married in December.

"I'll get back to you on that," Zoe said with a grin, closed her eyes, and went to sleep. It had been a good trip, and they were both glad they'd gone. And so was Charlie. Zoe had forgiven him, as much as she ever would. And he and Flavia had a son. Everything was finally right in the world.

# Chapter 17

Charlie and Darcy's divorce was final in December, and had gone smoothly. As he said he would, he had given her the house in the Hamptons, and the one in New York, and half the money he had been able to salvage after the bankruptcy. He couldn't pay her back for what he had done to her, but he at least wanted her to be comfortable and for nothing to change in her life or the girls'. He knew he was going to be all right in his new business and make back most of the money he had lost, maybe more. Department stores were dinosaurs, an online fashion business was the wave of the future, and he was going to catch that wave for Flavia and their son.

Charlie and Flavia were married in Rome on Christmas Eve, with her entire family present, and they christened their baby Umberto at the same time. The whole family felt her father's absence sorely, but they had a new life to celebrate, and Bianca's baby had been born two months before. Roberto walked Flavia down the aisle, and they both cried thinking of their father.

While the twins were in Rome for the wedding, Bill and Darcy went to Paris to spend a week with Sybille Carton. Darcy brought her the project she had been working on for months, a leather-bound book of her recipes, which Darcy had carefully noted and compiled. She had made a real book of them, and found a publisher for it. The cover of the book was a photograph of Sybille Carton at the height of her career as a movie star. The title was yet to be chosen by Sybille. The book was coming out in March, and Darcy handed her an envelope with the check that the publisher had paid as an advance. Mme. Carton's eyes grew wide when she saw the amount.

"You did this for me?"

"You taught me how to cook, and got me through the hardest month of my life, when my own life fell apart, and the whole world around us."

"You would have gotten through it anyway," Sybille said modestly, but she was visibly thrilled and deeply touched, as Bill smiled at them both.

His consulting business was getting off the ground, and he already had several big clients, including the government, who still wanted to use his services as an independent contractor, which had been a lucrative surprise.

Bill was happy he had taken the leap and retired from the CIA. It was time, and Mme. Carton had been right. About everything. About Darcy too.

He had moved to New York in September to start his new business, and had been staying with Darcy since the girls had left for B.U.

in the fall. He had gotten his own apartment so he could stay there when the girls came home for holidays, but the rest of the time he stayed with Darcy, and they had a wonderful time together. She was proud of him for setting up his own agency, and being brave enough to start a new life.

They arrived in Paris two days before Christmas Eve, when the girls flew to Rome for their father's wedding, and a big party the day before.

They had dinner with Mme. Carton on the first night. They were going to spend Christmas with her. She was the fairy godmother to their relationship, and stood in place of a mother to them both. They had decided to spend their first Christmas with her so she wouldn't be alone. They were staying in Darcy's old room, because it was a little bigger. And Sybille told Bill he could use his old room as a study if he needed it. The twins were spending Christmas with Charlie and Flavia after the wedding, and then going skiing with friends in Cortina when Charlie and Flavia left on their honeymoon to Tahiti the day after. They were taking the baby with them because Flavia was nursing. Her whole family had teased her and said she would probably come back from the honeymoon pregnant, since Umberto was already four months old. Flavia didn't tell them, but she thought she already was, and would have to stop nursing when she was sure. She couldn't wait to have another baby. The first one had been so easy, and Umberto was such a happy baby. They were crazy about him.

"So you're not a spy anymore, Bill?" Mme. Carton said with a smile, as Bill poured champagne for the three of them to celebrate her book. She was thrilled, and deeply grateful to Darcy. "And the two of you? Any plans?" She was fishing, and they smiled. She was happy to see them together, and that he had been brave enough to go after Darcy and not let her slip away. It had taken courage for him to reach out to her and make a life with her, and for Darcy to trust him, after all that had happened to her.

He didn't answer Sybille's question, but that night in Darcy's old room with the canopied bed, he turned to her, with a shy smile.

"Do we have plans?" he asked her.

"I don't know. Should we?" They had been living day to day and she was happy with him. Happier than she'd ever been. It was a good match, and the right fit for both.

"I think so," he said, and she smiled at him. He was solid and reliable, loving and strong, and an honorable man. He had proven it to her, and she knew she could count on him. They loved being together. The world had burned around them, and they had survived. Love had come from it, and new opportunities. Everything was new around them. Hope had been born again, and old dreams had been resurrected. Faith had been restored. One couldn't ask for more. They had proven that life could be new again, and even better than before. And others had found that to be true as well. After the terror and the nightmare came the resurrection, and the world was at peace again.

# About the Author

DANIELLE STEEL has been hailed as one of the world's bestselling authors, with a billion copies of her novels sold. Her many international bestsellers include *Only the Brave, Never Too Late, Upside Down, The Ball at Versailles, Second Act, Happiness, Palazzo,* and other highly acclaimed novels. She is also the author of *His Bright Light,* the story of her son Nick Traina's life and death; *A Gift of Hope,* a memoir of her work with the homeless; *Expect a Miracle,* a book of her favorite quotations for inspiration and comfort; *Pure Joy,* about the dogs she and her family have loved; and the children's books *Pretty Minnie in Paris* and *Pretty Minnie in Hollywood.*

daniellesteel.com
Facebook.com/DanielleSteelOfficial
X: @daniellesteel
Instagram: @officialdaniellesteel

## About the Type

This book was set in Charter, a typeface designed in 1987 by Matthew Carter (b. 1937) for Bitstream, Inc., a digital type-foundry that he cofounded in 1981. One of the most influential typographers of our time, Carter designed this versatile font to feature a compact width, squared serifs, and open letterforms. These features give the typeface a fresh, highly legible, and unencumbered appearance.